MONTANA MAVERICKS

Welcome to Big Sky Country, home of the Montana Mavericks, where free-spirited men and women discover love on the range.

THE REAL COWBOYS OF BRONCO HEIGHTS

The young people of Bronco are so busy with their careers—and their ranches— that they have pushed all thoughts of love to the back burner. Elderly Winona Cobbs knows full well what it's like to live a life that is only half full. And she resolves to help them see the error of their ways...

Dean Abernathy has been looking out for Susanna Henry since she was just a high school kid. Though she's twenty-five now, he is still protective of her. And now he believes the person she needs protection from is him. The world-weary cowboy thinks he is no match for Susanna's youth and imagination, and he's convinced that falling for her will only hold her back...

Dear Reader,

'Tis the season for twinkling lights and holiday treats and everything merry and bright!

In Bronco, Montana, it's also the season for the annual Christmas play. This year, the Bronco Theater Company is performing *A Christmas Wish*, written by—and starring—local thespian Susanna Henry.

Although my high school drama class was a long time ago, I remember how much work went into putting a show onstage—and it wasn't only the actors who labored under the lights. There were sets to be painted, costumes to be designed, music to be choreographed and lights to be focused. And in the weeks that preceded opening night, precious memories were made and lasting friendships forged.

Of course, Susanna is excited about the production of *A Christmas Wish*—and a little nervous, too. Because the story that she wrote for the stage is semi-autobiographical, and she's worried that Dean Abernathy, the hunky cowboy who's been her secret crush for almost as long as she's known him, might read between the lines spoken by the actors on stage and realize that she's in love with him.

Or maybe she's more worried that he *won't* read between the lines and will never see her as anything more than a friend.

But luck—or at least Mother Nature—is on her side. Stranded together in the empty theater during a winter blizzard, Dean finds himself getting up close and very personal with Susanna, and he begins to realize that it may be the season for falling in love...

I hope your heart is filled with love and joy this festive season and always!

Happy reading and happy holidays!

Brenda

Dreaming of a Christmas Cowboy

BRENDA HARLEN

HARLEQUIN
SPECIAL
EDITION

Special thanks and acknowledgment are given to
Brenda Harlen for her contribution to the Montana Mavericks:
The Real Cowboys of Bronco Heights miniseries.

HARLEQUIN®
SPECIAL
EDITION™

Recycling programs
for this product may
not exist in your area.

ISBN-13: 978-1-335-40821-1

Dreaming of a Christmas Cowboy

Copyright © 2021 by Harlequin Books S.A.

This edition published by arrangement with Harlequin Books S.A.

For questions and comments about the quality of this book,
please contact us at CustomerService@Harlequin.com.

Harlequin Enterprises ULC
22 Adelaide St. West, 40th Floor
Toronto, Ontario M5H 4E3, Canada
www.Harlequin.com

Printed in U.S.A.

Brenda Harlen is a former attorney who once had the privilege of appearing before the Supreme Court of Canada. The practice of law taught her a lot about the world and reinforced her determination to become a writer—because in fiction, she could promise a happy ending! Now she is an award-winning, RITA® Award–nominated, nationally bestselling author of more than fifty titles for Harlequin. You can keep up-to-date with Brenda on Facebook and Twitter, or through her website, brendaharlen.com.

Books by Brenda Harlen

Harlequin Special Edition

Match Made in Haven

The Sheriff's Nine-Month Surprise
Her Seven-Day Fiancé
Six Weeks to Catch a Cowboy
Claiming the Cowboy's Heart
Double Duty for the Cowboy
One Night with the Cowboy
A Chance for the Rancher
The Marine's Road Home
Meet Me Under the Mistletoe
The Rancher's Promise
The Chef's Surprise Baby

Montana Mavericks: The Real Cowboys of Bronco Heights

Dreaming of a Christmas Cowboy

Montana Mavericks: What Happened to Beatrix?

A Cowboy's Christmas Carol

Montana Mavericks: Six Brides for Six Brothers

Maverick Christmas Surprise

Montana Mavericks: The Lonelyhearts Ranch

Bring Me a Maverick for Christmas!

Visit the Author Profile page
at Harlequin.com for more titles.

For all the fabulous readers out there
who are "wild for Westerns from Harlequin."

Prologue

Eight years earlier

"Susanna? Are you in here?"

Susanna Henry froze at the sound of Dean Abernathy's voice.

Just when she'd thought the day couldn't get any worse…

She'd retreated to the copy room in the offices of Abernathy Meats to hide, because she knew she couldn't hold back the tears any longer. And the handsome cowboy was the absolute last person she wanted to see while her face was streaked with the remnants of her crying jag.

"Go away," she said.

She was humiliated enough without having to look at her boss's son with her heart in tatters.

"I'm not going away." His voice was patient but firm. "So you might as well tell me what's wrong."

She jabbed the buttons on the copier, then slid the pile of invoices into the feeder. "It's not important."

"Important enough to upset you," he countered, sounding reasonable and mature.

Because he was an adult—twenty-six to her seventeen—and if she wanted him to stop treating her like a child, she needed to stop acting like one.

"Fine," she decided. "If you must know, Scott dumped me."

The admission was followed by a sob, and her humiliation was complete.

Dean was quiet for a moment, and when he finally responded, his words weren't anything she might have anticipated.

"Well, that's a relief," he said.

Susanna turned then and looked at him through tear-filled eyes. "A relief?" she echoed.

"I'm not happy that you got dumped," Dean was quick to clarify. "But I'm glad that you're not with Scott anymore."

She blinked, trying to focus on him through her tears. "Why?"

He tipped her chin up and gently dabbed at her wet cheeks with a handkerchief.

What kind of cowboy carried a handkerchief?

The kind that a woman could count on to wipe her tears rather than cause them, she realized.

"Because he wasn't even close to being good enough for you," Dean told her, and the sincerity in his tone was a balm to her bruised and battered heart.

"We were supposed to go to California together. That's where we were going to make our dreams of Hollywood careers come true," she confided now, perhaps even more distraught about the change of plans than she was about being dumped. Because being an actress was all she'd wanted since she stood under the spotlight as one of "Thirteen Little Pigs"— a variation of "Three Little Pigs" that allowed everyone in her second-grade class to play a part.

"You are a strong, smart, beautiful woman," he said. "You don't need a man to make your dreams come true."

Susanna appreciated his faith in her.

And, even more important, she realized he was right.

She didn't need a man—especially not one like Scott Thompson.

Too bad the only other man who'd ever made her heart beat a little too fast had never treated her like anything but a kid sister.

Chapter One

Present day

The towering evergreen in front of City Hall had been wrapped in hundreds—maybe thousands—of colorful lights, and Susanna couldn't wait to see it illuminated. Of course, she wasn't the only one. Bronco's Annual Christmas Tree Lighting, sponsored by local merchants and craft vendors, was a community event that had a way of bringing everyone together.

As she'd wandered through the crowd earlier, she'd spotted local rancher Jameson John and his fiancée, Vanessa Cruise; rodeo star Geoff Burris and his fiancée, Stephanie Brandt; and Sofia Sanchez with Boone Dalton, the cowboy who'd stolen her heart. It seemed as if love was in the air in Bronco, and though Susanna was pleased for all the happy couples milling around, she was beginning to despair of ever finding her own real-life happily-ever-after.

On the stage, she'd had several leading men fall in love with her—or at least the character she was playing in that moment. Under the lights, she was a woman who commanded interest and attention. But when she walked out of the theater at the end of the night, she was simply Susanna Henry again—office manager by day, community actor by night, twenty-five years old and alone.

You don't need a man to make your dreams come true.

Dean Abernathy's long-ago words had become something of a mantra for Susanna, and she really did believe they were true. But she couldn't deny that she wanted a partner to share her life and her hopes and her dreams, someone to love and who would love her in return. As she bore witness to so many of her friends and neighbors falling in love, getting married and having babies—not necessarily in that order—Susanna's desire for a family of her own continued to grow stronger.

She pushed the thought aside as Daphne Cruise—another newlywed and also the owner and operator of Happy Hearts Animal Sanctuary—appeared on the stage with Maggie, the dog firmly attached to the end of a red leash. In honor of the season, the Australian shepherd/border collie mix—winner of the coveted crown awarded to "Bronco's Favorite Pet" at the Fourth of July festival—was decked out in a Santa hat and jingle bells. The crowd cheered, happy to see that the missing pooch had been safely returned to the rescue shelter, thanks to numerous tips from the public.

"I want to thank everyone who emailed or called

to share their Maggie sightings over the past several months," Daphne said. "And especially Boone Dalton, who ultimately brought this beautiful girl back to Happy Hearts. As a result, Maggie is once again looking forward to a happy future with her adoptive family—" she paused to allow the applause to die down "—but not just yet, because our adventurous pooch is soon going to be a mommy!"

Of course, that announcement brought another round of cheers that made Daphne's smile grow even wider.

"Boone," she said, zeroing in on the man in the audience, "you can have your pick of the litter, if you want. Everyone else will have to go through the usual application process. Puppies are always popular, but remember, if your application isn't chosen this time, we have other dogs and cats looking for good homes."

"Thank you for that public service announcement," the mayor said, taking back the microphone.

Susanna listened with half an ear, her gaze scanning the crowd as the mayor continued talking. She was unsurprised to see that most of the Abernathy family was in attendance, seated in the front rows that were always reserved for VIPs, including Hutch and Hannah, and three of their five sons: Weston, Crosby and Dean.

Susanna's traitorous heart gave a happy little skip when she spotted Dean, but she determinedly ignored it as she continued her perusal. She didn't see

Dean's older brother, Garrett, and suspected that he'd made up some excuse to stay back at the ranch. His youngest brother, Tyler, had a ready excuse in his now thirteen-month-old daughter, Maeve, but Susanna suspected that if she looked hard enough, she'd find Tyler somewhere in the crowd with his daughter and his fiancée, Callie Sheldrick.

But she didn't look too hard, as her gaze kept drifting back to Dean. The second-born of Hutch and Hannah Abernathy's five sons, Dean was eight years younger than forty-two-year-old Garrett. Apparently, when several years passed after their eldest son's birth without Hannah getting pregnant again, she and her husband had begun to think they might only ever have one child. But eventually Dean came along, then Weston two years after Dean, and Crosby two years after Weston, and finally Tyler, another two years later.

Working at Abernathy Meats, Susanna had gotten to know all of them—and numerous Abernathy cousins, too—quite well, and she was fond of each one. But from the beginning, there had been something about Dean that drew her. And whatever that something was, it continued to have the same effect.

Though his brothers were every bit as handsome and charming, there was something about Dean's presence that made her heart beat just a little bit faster whenever she was near him. Not that she had any intention of letting him know it.

Because Dean had never treated her like anything

but a little sister. He teased her as readily as he teased his siblings, but he was protective of her in a way he wouldn't dare be with his brothers.

She hadn't minded so much when she was seventeen. In fact, she would have been mortified if he'd guessed she had a secret crush on him when she started working in the office at Abernathy Meats. Especially since she'd been certain that her crush would fade over time.

Unfortunately, it had not. If anything, her feelings for the handsome cowboy had only grown stronger. Even more unfortunate was the fact that he continued to look at her as if she was a teenager rather than a grown woman, with a woman's dreams and desires.

"Now I have the sincere pleasure of announcing the title of this year's Christmas play," the mayor continued. "The Bronco Theater Company will be performing *A Christmas Wish*, written by our very own star of the stage, Susanna Henry.

"Susanna, would you like to come up here and tell everyone a little bit more about the holiday production?"

Roused from her thoughts of Dean, she stepped up and accepted the proffered microphone.

"Thank you, Mister Mayor, for that gracious introduction. I'm so excited to be part of the fabulous group of people bringing *A Christmas Wish* to the stage for all of you this holiday season.

"This play is a family-friendly holiday romance starring myself as Holly—because yes, she who writes the play gets to claim the lead." She waited for the laughter to fade before she continued, "But seriously, it's the rest of the cast that truly makes this the not-to-be-missed event of the season and I'm honored to introduce them to you now.

"Marty Trujillo as the love interest; Avery Lang as the best friend; Roger Perrin as the college buddy; Liz Crockett as the nosy neighbor; plus a special guest appearance by Santa Claus himself. And last but certainly not least, I'd like to introduce the man in charge of putting it all together—our director, Charles Russet."

Polite applause followed the announcement of each name, and the respective actors bowed an acknowledgment to the crowd as they joined her onstage.

"Tickets are on sale now at the Bronco Theater Company booth with proceeds being divided among local charities," Susanna said. "I look forward to seeing you all at the theater."

Obviously pleased by the enthusiastic response, Marty wrapped his arms around Susanna and spun her in a circle, delighting the crowd.

"A sneak preview of better things to come," he promised the audience with an exaggerated wink, before hooking his arm with that of his costar and leading her away.

"Always trying to upstage me, aren't you?" she said, as they walked away from the crowd, still arm in arm.

"Never," he denied, with an easy grin.

But she knew that he could. Marty was an incredibly talented actor—with actual Broadway experience—and she felt lucky that he'd even shown an interest in being part of the Bronco holiday production.

"Do you miss the bright lights and the big city?" she asked, as they made their way toward the concession booths to join the line of people waiting for cups of hot apple cider.

"Not really," he said. "And when I do, I hop on a plane to New York for a few days—and then I come home again, grateful for the life I have here."

"I went to New York once," she told him.

"Did you love it or hate it?"

She smiled. "Are those the only two options?"

He shrugged. "In my experience, people have very strong reactions to the city—one way or the other."

"I loved it," she said. "I woke up every morning of the four days that I was there and stood in line for discount theater tickets, determined to see as many plays and shows as I could, and I was never disappointed. The talent was unbelievable. Not just on Broadway, but off-Broadway and off-off-Broadway."

"Add a couple more *offs*, and you might have been in one of the theaters where I performed," he noted dryly.

She nudged him with her shoulder. "Now I know you're just being modest, because Chuck told me that you've done a couple of off-Broadway productions."

He rolled his eyes. "Minor roles."

"Still," she said.

"It was an unforgettable experience," he acknowledged. "Though there are some parts of my life in the Big Apple that I wish I could forget."

"Like what?" she wondered.

"Sharing a one-bedroom apartment with two roommates because none of us could afford a place on our own. Eating questionable leftover takeout because auditions and rehearsals and voice lessons and dance classes often didn't leave time for a trip to the grocery store."

"I guess the starving artist thing isn't just a myth."

"And no matter how well a show is received, applause doesn't pay the rent or put food on the table."

"But you followed your dream," she said, her voice a little wistful.

He nodded. "I did. And now I teach drama at the local high school."

"Which you love."

"Which I don't hate," he acknowledged.

"You also started a summer theater camp for budding child actors," she noted.

"And other kids who lack the athleticism for sports camps."

"You're horrible," she chided, fighting the smile that wanted to curve her lips.

"I'm honest," he said.

"My point is, you followed your dream," she said again.

"And I still am," he confided.

That gave her pause.

"You're not going back to New York," she said. "At least not before the New Year, right?"

She must have sounded as panicked as she felt at the prospect of losing her leading man less than three weeks before opening night, because Marty chuckled.

"I'm not going anywhere," he promised.

"Then what did you mean about still following your dreams?" she wondered.

"Just that dreams change over time," he said. "And I've traded in the spotlight for potlights."

"I'm still confused," she admitted.

"We bought a house. Me and Brian. And the bank."

She smiled easily now. "That's exciting."

"And more than a little scary," he admitted. "But we wanted to have a home of our own before we started a family."

Susanna was happy for her costar, and perhaps a little bit envious. Because her dreams had changed over the years, too, and though she no longer dreamed of seeing her name on a theater marquee, her desire for a family of her own remained elusive.

"You're looking awfully serious all of a sudden," Marty remarked, as they inched toward the front of the line.

She sighed. "I guess I was just wondering why it seems so easy to pen happy endings for my characters when my own continues to be out of reach."

"You're just a babe in the woods," her costar said. "You should be thinking about beginnings, not endings."

"I'm twenty-five," she told him.

"Like I said—a babe in the woods." Marty paid for two cups of cider, then handed one to Susanna.

She studied him over the rim of her cup as she blew on the steaming liquid. "How old are you?"

He lifted his brows, a smile playing at the corners of his mouth. "How old do you think I am?"

She'd already given the matter some thought. He had a lot of theater experience, but his youthful look—and outlook—made it difficult to guess his actual age.

But she decided to take a shot. "Thirty?"

The hint of a smile gave way to a full grin. "Oh, sweetie, I love you for that."

"Not thirty," she realized.

He looked around, as if to ensure no one was close enough to overhear, but still whispered close to her ear, "Thirty-seven."

She was genuinely surprised by his response, but she couldn't resist responding playfully, "You certainly don't act your age."

"I'm an actor," he reminded her with a wink. "I can act whatever age I want, and I don't want to be closer to forty than thirty."

She couldn't help but laugh. "Do you really think that attitude's going to prevent Brian from tucking you away at Snowy Mountain when your time comes?" she teased, referring to Bronco's residence for seniors.

"Since I'm only four months older than Brian, maybe we'll tuck away there together," he said, as Susanna lifted a hand in response to a friend's wave.

Marty followed the direction of her gaze. "Who's that?"

"You've lived in Bronco for almost two years now, so you must have been to Bronco Java and Juice," she said.

"Of course."

"Well, that's the owner—Cassidy Ware," she said. "With her former high school sweetheart now fiancé, Brandon Taylor."

"I swear there must be something in the water in this town," Marty mused. "Something that might explain why so many people have been getting engaged and married and having babies in the past couple of years."

Susanna wished the explanation was that simple. But despite drinking a lot of water, she was still husbandless and childless, forcing her to acknowledge that those things might never happen for her.

Yes, she was only twenty-five years old, but considering that she hadn't had a serious relationship since she broke up with Scott Thompson in their senior year of high school, she didn't hold out a lot of hope of finding matrimonial bliss in her future. Sure, she dated. Fairly regularly, in fact. But she'd recently realized the problem wasn't with any of the men she dated but with herself.

Because she'd given her heart away a long time ago and hadn't ever managed to take it back.

Dean Abernathy ignored the sound of his two brothers chattering like magpies, his focus on Susanna Henry, walking arm in arm with her costar.

"Someone's forgetting the cardinal rule for this time of year," Crosby remarked.

"Better not pout?" Weston guessed.

Dean was only half listening, but he caught an answering nod out of the corner of his eye.

"You better watch out, big brother," Crosby said warningly. "Or you'll wake up to coal in your stocking on Christmas morning."

Dean tore his gaze away from Susanna to glance at his brothers. "What are you two blathering on about?"

"Santa Claus is coming to town," Weston said.

"I've heard the rumors," he acknowledged dryly.

"And yet, you're walking around with a scowl on your face."

"Almost a pout," Crosby added.

"I'm not scowling," Dean denied, making an effort to smooth out his brow. "And I'm definitely not pouting."

"You're also not smiling, and this is supposed to be a festive occasion."

"I just don't understand why people make such a fuss over lighting a tree," he muttered.

"Because it's Christmas," Crosby said. "And because you know the residents of this town love any excuse to get together to celebrate."

"Never mind that there are things that need to be done back at the ranch."

"You were perfectly happy to be here, chowing down on ribs from DJ's booth, until you saw Susanna Henry's costar get up close and personal," Weston noted. "Then your hackles rose like a guard dog sensing a threat."

"So you thought he was inappropriate, too?" Dean latched on to that part of his brother's statement with relief, because it validated his own feelings.

"Actually, no, I didn't," Weston told him. "And if Susanna had an issue, she would have handled it. She's a grown woman, more than capable of taking care of herself."

He was right, Dean acknowledged.

But when had that happened?

When had Susanna gone from being a high school senior, whose tears he'd dried, to an attractive woman who drew admiring glances as she made her way through the crowd on the arm of her costar?

And why did the sudden realization that she was all grown up make him uneasy?

His gaze drifted back to her again.

Despite the chill in the air, the long black coat she wore was unbuttoned to reveal a blue sweater with a reindeer head on the front—actual bells on its antlers and a fluffy red pom-pom for its nose. She'd paired the ridiculous sweater with dark jeans that hugged her shapely curves and black boots with a sexy little heel. She was smiling and laughing, obviously having a good time with her costar.

"What do you know about this Marty guy?" Dean asked his brothers.

"Just about as much as you do," Weston said.

"Same." Crosby nodded. "Although Roger could probably tell you more," he said, referring to the man who'd been a friend since grade school. "Considering that he's part of the cast."

"That was a surprise to me," Dean remarked. "I didn't know he was interested in theater."

Weston snorted. "He's not half as interested in theater as he is in our local playwright."

"Susanna?"

"She'd be the one," Crosby confirmed, as Weston abruptly abandoned his brothers to intercept a pretty female who'd caught his eye.

Dean scowled. "You're saying that Roger is in the play because he likes Susanna?"

"And also because he's got some talent. But yeah, he actually tried out for the role of Noel—and he was really disappointed when it went to Marty Trujillo."

"Why did he want to play Noel?" Dean wondered.

"Because Noel gets to kiss Holly."

"Who's Holly?"

Now Crosby rolled his eyes. "The character played by Susanna."

"I thought this was supposed to be a family-friendly play," Dean grumbled.

"It's just a kiss," Crosby said. "Not a hot and heavy make-out session. But Roger was hoping that if they spent a lot of time together during rehearsals, one thing might lead to another."

"Isn't Susanna a little young for Roger?"

"He's the same age as me," thirty-year-old Crosby noted.

"Exactly my point," Dean said.

"And Susanna's not seventeen anymore," his brother reminded him.

Dean knew exactly how old she was, because they'd had a cake for her at Abernathy Meats to celebrate her quarter-century milestone. But despite knowing how old she was, she still seemed younger to him. Certainly too young for Roger Perrin.

"Are you saying that you'd be okay with your friend dating Susanna?" he asked skeptically.

"Why wouldn't I be? I like Susanna and I like Roger."

"Because it's *Susanna*," Dean said, as if that explained anything.

"Who happens to be a beautiful, sexy, strong, confident woman."

His gaze narrowed. "It sounds like Roger isn't the only one who has his eye on our office manager."

"I don't have my eye on Susanna," Crosby assured him. "But I do have eyes in my head, and if you can't see that Susanna has a lot to offer, then you're not looking."

"Of course I'm not looking," Dean said. "Because we're talking about *Susanna.*"

"You keep emphasizing her name, as if to remind yourself that she's off-limits," his brother remarked, sounding amused.

"I'm not the one who apparently needs a reminder that she's off-limits—or should be."

"Why?" Crosby asked. "And you don't get to say, 'because she's Susanna' again."

So Dean said nothing.

"And if you're so certain you're not interested, then you don't get to be pissed when someone else is."

"I'm only looking out for her," Dean said, almost certain it was true.

Because it wasn't possible that he could be interested in Susanna.

No, it wasn't possible at all.

Chapter Two

On their way back toward the big tree in front of City Hall, Susanna and Marty had no choice but to come to an abrupt halt when a woman stepped directly into their path. Though Winona Cobbs had only moved to Bronco the previous winter, she was already something of a legend in town. A self-proclaimed psychic who'd opened up her Wisdom by Winona shop alongside her great-grandson's ghost tour business over the summer, she did not dress to blend with the crowd.

Today the nonagenarian was wearing a cherry red winter coat that fell to her knees, a knitted purple hat with a fat pom-pom on the top that tipped drunkenly to one side, bright lime-green mittens and purple boots. The deep lines of her face attested to her age, but her eyes were bright and curious, and despite holding the handle of a flowered quad cane fitted with steel prongs to help her safely navigate the snowy—and possibly icy—terrain, she'd been moving at a pretty good pace when she stepped in front of them.

"I'm looking forward to seeing your play," Winona Cobbs said, speaking to Susanna.

"I'm happy to hear that," she replied, with a cautious smile.

"They say that life imitates art," Winona continued, "but sometimes I wonder if it isn't really the other way around."

Goose bumps rose on Susanna's skin. "What do you mean by that?"

She'd never really believed the rumors about the old woman's psychic abilities, but now she found herself wondering if Winona might somehow know what—or who—had been on Susanna's mind (and in her heart!) while she worked on the script.

"A good writer can find stories everywhere," the old woman mused aloud, not actually answering the question. "But sometimes stories need revision."

Now Susanna was even more confused. "Are you telling me that my play needs work?"

Winona's smile was secretive. "How would I know? I haven't had the opportunity to read it, have I?"

"No," Susanna admitted. Although it wasn't outside the realm of possibility to think that she might have got her hands on a copy of the script. All the actors had copies, as did almost everyone else involved in the production. Or maybe the old woman had sneaked into the theater to watch part of a rehearsal. With so many people coming and going, it didn't make sense to lock the doors of the theater during rehearsals.

"Well, I have read it," Marty chimed in. "And I can assure you, it's wonderful."

Winona narrowed her gaze on Susanna's costar. "You know how to play to an audience, don't you? But you're not so good an actor that you can convince me you have a romantic interest in Miss Henry."

"I'm wounded," he said, dramatically splaying a hand over his chest.

"Poppycock." The old woman's tone was dismissive, but her eyes sparkled with humor. "But you don't need to worry that you'll wound her heart, because it belongs to another."

"Does it, now?" Marty asked, sounding curious.

"And that's all I'm going to say on the matter," Winona told him firmly. "But I also wanted to express my hope that this holiday—and Miss Henry's production—will be the best one yet."

"Thank you," Susanna murmured, feeling more than a little unnerved by the encounter.

The old woman nodded to her and moved along.

"She's every bit as odd as people say, isn't she?" Marty remarked, watching her walk away.

Odd was one word for Winona, and possibly one of the more charitable ones, Susanna thought. Though, of course, she didn't say so aloud.

"If even half of what I've heard is true, she's been through a lot in her ninety-plus years," Susanna said. "It might be that her…eccentric behavior is simply a result of her life experience."

"Or maybe she really *is* psychic," Marty suggested. "If you believe in that sort of thing."

"Do you?" she asked curiously.

He shrugged. "I'm open to the possibility."

Her discomfort must have shown on her face, because he laughed.

"I take it you're not?"

"I prefer my reality to be grounded in reality," she told him.

"I think the idea that someone might be able to see things you can't—or don't want to—scares you."

"Poppycock," she said, mimicking the old woman's indignant tone.

He grinned. "Then you wouldn't object to visiting Wisdom by Winona with me sometime?"

"So she can trace a finger over my palm and tell me that my true love is out there, I just have to be patient?"

"Are you growing impatient?" he asked.

"Only to see the tree lit up," she said, because she had no intention of discussing her lack of a love life with her costar.

Again.

One minute, the evergreen was a towering silhouette in the darkness, then the mayor flipped a switch, and the tree was ablaze with countless red, yellow, green and blue lights. The crowd gasped, then broke into enthusiastic applause and one of the local high school choirs began to sing "O Christmas Tree."

Marty took off immediately after the ceremonial lighting, but Susanna remained to enjoy the lights and the music. A short while later, Dean joined her.

"A lot of people are buzzing about your Christmas production," he told her.

"Really?" She couldn't help but feel pleased by this revelation.

"Did you not see the line at the booth for tickets?"

"Actually no, I didn't," she admitted, craning her neck to look now, though it was impossible to see anything through the crowd.

"You seem to have a solid cast again this year," Dean said. "Although that Marty guy seems a little... handsy."

Marty?

Handsy?

Susanna nearly laughed out loud at the ridiculousness of the characterization.

"Because he hugged me onstage?"

"Well, yeah," Dean said. "It didn't seem entirely appropriate."

"He's Noel to my Holly," she said. "Which makes his action entirely appropriate."

"So you're like...romantic partners?"

"Onstage, yes."

Dean's brows drew together. "Who did the casting? Because he looks like he's my age—which makes him way too old for you."

"Does age really matter when two people are in love?" she countered.

His scowl deepened. "Now you're telling me that you're in love with him?"

"No, I'm telling you that Holly's in love with

Noel—and he's in love with her," she explained patiently. "And if you want to know anything more than that, you'll have to buy a ticket to see the play."

"You know that no one in the Abernathy family will miss it."

She did know. Dean and his brothers and their parents had always been supportive of the theater—and of Susanna. Hutch and Hannah had given her a job when she was barely seventeen, offering flexible hours that accommodated her school schedule and drama club commitments. In the beginning, she'd saved every penny from her paycheck for her intended trip to California. Then, when her plans with Scott fell through, she'd continued working at Abernathy Meats because she didn't see any reason not to.

Though she'd started out as a part-time receptionist, she'd eventually been promoted through the ranks to full-time office manager. Maybe it wasn't quite the path that Susanna had planned for her life, but she wasn't unhappy. She enjoyed her job and she liked the people she worked with, and her involvement with the community theater satisfied her acting bug.

Lately, however, she'd found herself wanting more. In particular, she wished for a partner to share her life—someone to love and who would love her. But in the meantime, at least the characters she played on the stage got their happy endings.

As she was preoccupied with her musing, she saw Roger extricate himself from a group of friends and make his way over.

"I'm going to grab a cup of hot cider. Can I get one for you, Susanna?" he asked, ignoring the man standing by her side.

"No, thanks. I'm good."

"I'm good, too," Dean said, though Roger was already gone.

Susanna couldn't help but chuckle at the pique in the cowboy's tone.

"Did you come here with him?" he asked her now.

"Roger?"

Dean nodded.

"Yeah. The whole cast came over together after rehearsal."

"So...not a date?"

"Not a date," she confirmed, intrigued by the un-characteristic brusqueness of his tone.

"That's good."

She sent him a quizzical glance.

"Because it would probably be awkward to get involved with someone you have to work with," he explained.

"Probably," she agreed. But she'd quit her job in a heartbeat if Dean ever showed the slightest bit of romantic interest. Which, unfortunately, he had not.

"In the theater, I mean," he added, to clarify his previous statement.

She nodded, wondering why the man who'd been a good friend for several years was suddenly acting awkward and uncomfortable around her.

"Is everything okay?"

"Yeah." He stuffed his hands in his pockets. "I was just thinking that it's getting late. I should be heading back to the ranch."

"Okay," she said agreeably.

But still, Dean hesitated.

"Did you need a ride home?" he finally asked.

Because that was Dean—always looking out for her.

She shook her head. "Thanks, but my car's at the theater."

"Then I'll walk you to your car."

"That's not necessary."

"I'm not going to let you walk all the way over there by yourself in the dark," he said.

"It isn't that far." She didn't point out that it wasn't up to him to *let her* do anything, because she knew his heart was in the right place.

And firmly out of her reach.

"It's far enough."

She bit back a sigh. "But I'm not ready to go just yet."

"Then I'll wait until you are ready," he said.

"You know what? Roger's parked at the theater, too, so I'll walk over with him later."

"What makes you think you'll be safe with Roger?"

She huffed out an impatient breath. "Because I know Roger."

"You know me better," he said.

It was true.

And because she knew him so well, she knew that he could be like a dog with a bone when he got an idea in his head.

She sighed. "Okay, then. Let's go."

Because if he was determined to look out for her—and apparently he was—there was no way she was going to stop him.

And why would she even try?

"Something smells good," Joyce Henry said, coming into the kitchen late Sunday afternoon, when she returned home from her shift as a clerk at Bronco Drugs & Sundries.

"I've got sugar cookies in the oven," Susanna said, as she finished washing the bowls and utensils she'd used to mix the dough.

"Are you going to share?" her mom asked hopefully. "Or are they all for your theater friends?"

"I made them to take to rehearsal tomorrow night, but I'll leave some here," she promised.

"You've been doing a lot of baking lately," Joyce remarked, lowering herself into a chair and lifting her feet onto the seat of another.

"'Tis the season," she said.

"'Tis the season to gain back those ten pounds you lost, if you're not careful," her mom warned.

"I'm being careful," she said.

At least, she was *trying* to be careful.

And if she'd already gained back three of those

pounds, she was still down seven, which was a win in her book.

"I think you look fabulous," Joyce said now. "I'm only trying to be supportive because you said you wanted to lose a few more pounds."

Actually, she wanted to lose another ten—or maybe even fifteen—but if she admitted as much to her mother, Joyce would worry that Susanna was too preoccupied with a number on the scale.

She knew her mom only wanted good things for her and was always cheering for Susanna to succeed—so long as her daughter's aspirations were the kind that Joyce approved of.

And becoming a professional actor wasn't.

Of course, Joyce had good reasons for not wanting to lose her daughter to Tinseltown, too.

While Susanna was in high school and planning her California adventure with Scott, she'd been excited about the possibility of reconnecting with Ron Henry—the father she hadn't seen in several years. Seduced by the glamor of Hollywood, the former ranch hand had left his wife and child in Bronco to pursue a career in movies. And he'd had some success, albeit as a stunt double rather than a marquee actor.

But when she'd called him and told him of her plans, he hadn't been nearly as enthusiastic as she'd hoped.

"Everyone should follow their dreams," he'd told her. "But people need to be realistic, too."

"You don't think I've got the talent?" she'd guessed.

"Your mom's sent me enough tapes of your performances that I know you can act. But Hollywood is more discerning than high school, and it would be a mistake to expect that you'll ever be cast as anything more than the chubby best friend."

The blunt remark had stunned Susanna, and even eight years later, the memory of his words still stung.

"Is that how you see me?" she'd asked her father.

"It's not about how I see you," Ron had denied. "It's about how casting directors are going to see you."

Unfortunately, she knew he was right—because of what happened with *The Wizard of Oz*. And his words were all it took to transport Susanna back to seventh grade and the middle school gymnatorium where auditions had been held to cast the roles.

Susanna had nailed her audition. She'd been certain of it. And she'd been so eager to share her excitement with her mom that she'd raced out of the gymnatorium without her backpack. When she returned for the forgotten book bag a short while later, the three teachers in charge of casting had still been seated at the table facing the stage, discussing the actors in their effort to assign roles.

Susanna had closed the door quietly, so as not to interrupt, and tiptoed over to the bench along the side wall where she'd left her bag. She wasn't trying to eavesdrop, but there was no way she couldn't overhear them talking. And maybe she did linger a little longer when she realized they were talking about *her*.

"Did you hear Susanna Henry sing? Such a stunning voice," Miss Fitzgerald said. "If you closed your eyes, you'd almost swear she was Judy Garland."

"You'd have to close your eyes," Mr. Dekker said.

"What's that supposed to mean?" Miss Fitzgerald demanded, a definite edge to her tone.

"You know very well what it means," Mr. Dekker said. "We can't have a Dorothy who's wider than the Cowardly Lion."

"It would be easy enough to add padding to the lion costume," Ms. Trevino said, attempting to find middle ground.

"It would be even easier to cast Susanna as the lion and Alicia Krecji as Dorothy."

"Alicia has a decent voice," Miss Fitzgerald acknowledged. "But in last year's play, she only showed up to half the rehearsals."

Susanna didn't stick around to hear any more.

And when the casting list was posted, she saw that she'd been cast as the cowardly lion.

Alicia Krecji got the role of Dorothy.

It had been a harsh lesson, but perhaps a necessary one.

But Susanna had learned (with the help of a counselor her mom had found) to not just accept but also appreciate her body, because she was fit even if she wasn't thin. And despite what she'd later refer to as "The Dorothy Setback," she regularly won major

roles in seasonal productions in high school, where
Miss Fitzgerald's sister was head of the department.
It was through her involvement with the drama club
that she'd gotten to know Scott Thompson. They
spent a lot of time together, working on various productions through the years, and had eventually—
perhaps inevitably—fallen in love.

Their plan to get married after graduation and
move to LA to work in the entertainment industry
was a long shot, Susanna knew, but it was a shot she
wanted to take—especially with Scott by her side.
But when she told him what her dad had said, he'd
agreed that she'd probably have to take off some
weight if she was going to compete for starring roles
in LA—as if the extra pounds were as easy to shed
as a costume.

Still, Scott was supportive of her—until they
broke up in their senior year. That was when her
dream of a life and career in Hollywood slipped
through her fingers.

It didn't help Susanna's self-confidence any to
learn that, not three weeks after the breakup, her ex
had hooked up with Mara Hemingway, who probably weighed one hundred pounds soaking wet. Next
to Mara, Susanna had always felt too big, too loud,
too everything. And since a lot of their teachers in
both elementary and secondary school liked to assign seats alphabetically, Susanna frequently found
herself next to Mara.

Maybe she shouldn't have given up on her California dream, but she wasn't brave enough to go so far away from home on her own. Instead, she opted to stay in Bronco and go to community college, which allowed her to continue working at Abernathy Meats. Four years later, she had a business management degree and several college drama productions to add to her theatrical résumé.

After finishing college, she'd decided it was time to move out of her childhood home. She'd even put in an application at BH247—an upscale apartment complex in Bronco Heights. Joyce hadn't said a word to discourage her, but when Susanna got the call offering her a unit in the coveted building, she'd surprised herself as much as the property manager by turning it down. Because it had been just Susanna and her mom for most of her life, and she couldn't imagine leaving her alone in the house on Cottonwood Crescent.

She wasn't unhappy with her decision to stay in Bronco. She just wanted more than her office job and a semiannual stage production. She wanted a family—a man to love who loved her back, and children of her own whose dreams she would nurture.

She'd had boyfriends since Scott, of course, although none that she'd cared about as much as she cared about him. But maybe that was her fault. Maybe she was afraid to open her heart and risk having it trampled again.

And why wouldn't she be when every man she'd

ever met—including, or maybe especially, her father—had let her down?

Every man except Dean Abernathy.

Well, Dean's brothers had proven themselves to be stand-up guys, too, but Dean was the only one that she'd had a secret crush on for the better part of the eight years that she'd known him.

Not that he had a clue, and she was grateful for that.

Grateful—and a little frustrated, too, that despite the fact that they'd become friends, he continued to treat her as if she was a kid.

Or, even worse, a sister.

But over the years, as she watched him go out with other women, she'd always felt confident that the day would come when he'd realize that he was wasting his time with them, because he was in love with her.

A secret hope that had been dealt a near fatal blow when Dean proposed to Whitney St. George.

Susanna had been devastated to see the gorgeous brunette parading around with Dean's ring on her finger. And during the course of the engagement, Whitney had spent a lot of time hanging around the office, talking wedding plans with her future in-laws, discussing where she and Dean would live, the kind of house they'd build and the number of children they would have.

Susanna wanted him to be happy, she truly did.

But she wanted him to be happy with *her*.

Somehow, though, she managed to be polite to

Whitney. She even gave her opinion on fonts for wedding invitations when asked by the bride-to-be, and she smiled through gritted teeth as debate raged over the choice of peonies or ranunculus for the bridal bouquet.

Despite all her meticulous research and careful planning, there was one thing that Whitney couldn't get Dean to commit to: a wedding date. And that, of course, stalled everything else. Because until they settled on a date (preferably in June, because she'd always dreamed of a summer wedding but July and August were too hot—a bride wanted to glow with happiness, not glisten with sweat), they couldn't book the church (All Saints, because the Abernathy family were members) or a reception venue (The Association, of course, because nothing less than the most exclusive place in town would do) or music (a string quartet to play during the meal, followed by a popular local country band for dancing) or—

The details that Whitney went on and on about made Susanna's head spin, though she knew that wasn't the fault of Dean's fiancée but the simple fact that Whitney *was* Dean's fiancée. Because when Dean got married, when he stood up in front of his family and friends and promised to love, honor and cherish the gorgeous brunette in the size four dress, then Susanna would finally have to give up the last, lingering hope that the sexy cowboy was secretly, hopelessly in love with her.

Then the engagement was called off, and Susanna

couldn't help but feel sad for Dean, who'd obviously cared deeply for Whitney. At the same time, she'd felt an overwhelming sense of relief, as her secret hopes of a happy-ever-after for herself and the handsome cowboy were able to soar freely once again.

Three years later, Susanna was still working at Abernathy Meats. Still going out on dates she knew would lead nowhere. Still secretly wishing that Dean would look at her the way a man looks at a woman he wants. And still dreaming of him when she was alone in her bed at night.

Chapter Three

Dean walked into his parents' house, hung his coat and Stetson on a hook by the back door, then lowered himself onto the wooden bench to remove his boots before making his way to the kitchen. His mom was standing at the island, the makings of a salad spread out in front of her.

He dipped his head to kiss her cheek. "Am I the first one here?"

"Actually, you're the last one here," she told him. "It's just you and me and your dad tonight."

"Where's everyone else?"

"Garrett had some stuff he said he wanted to do at home, Callie was making dinner for Tyler and Maeve, and Crosby and Weston went into town to meet some friends at Doug's bar." She finished slicing the cucumber and glanced up at him then. "Didn't they invite you to join them?"

"Weston did say something about it," Dean said, remembering now. "I just wasn't in the mood to go into town."

"Are you in the mood for lasagna? Because that's what's in the oven."

His stomach growled its approval. "Do I smell garlic bread, too?"

"Don't I always serve garlic bread with pasta?"

He nodded. And salad was another staple in her kitchen—which was why she was chopping up vegetables.

"Can I give you a hand?" Dean offered.

"Yeah, you can grab a couple of beers and go hang out with your dad in the living room," she said. "I don't need you underfoot while I'm getting things ready."

Dean did as he was told, walking past the dining room to the living room, where his dad was watching television.

"Thanks," Hutch said, accepting the bottle of beer his son proffered.

"Why does Mom have the table set with her good dishes?" he asked, settling on the opposite end of the sofa.

His dad shrugged. "You know she likes to take them out every now and again. Says there's no point in having them if we're not going to use them."

It was true, and yet Dean couldn't shake the feeling that he was missing something.

"Is it a special occasion?"

"Nah," Hutch said, even as a slight tinge of pink colored his cheeks.

"It is," he realized. But he knew it wasn't her birthday or their anniversary. "What did I miss?"

"You didn't miss anything," his dad assured him,

even as the pink color deepened. "It's just…date night at home."

"Date night at home?" Dean echoed.

"It's something we started doing years ago, when you boys were little. When we didn't have the energy— or the money, to be honest—to go out, we'd have date night at home."

"You can afford to take her out somewhere nice now," he pointed out to his dad.

"And I do on occasion," Hutch promised. "But these quiet nights at home kind of became our thing, and your mom still enjoys them."

"And I'm intruding."

"You're not."

"You don't need a third wheel on date night."

"Date night doesn't start until after dinner," his dad said. "You think we didn't feed our kids before we popped the corn and slid a favorite movie into the VCR?"

"I hope you've at least moved on to DVDs some-time in the last two decades," Dean remarked.

"We had to—after you and your brothers gave us a Blu-ray player for our anniversary several years back," Hutch acknowledged.

"So…popcorn and a movie—that's Mom's idea of date night?"

"Well—" his dad cleared his throat "—she likes to cuddle, too."

He wanted to tease his dad about the lame date night plans, but truthfully, Dean thought that popcorn and a movie with someone special sounded pretty great.

Whitney had preferred to be out with other people. In fact, he couldn't honestly recall if he'd ever seen a movie with his former fiancée. But for the past several years, since he'd discovered that Susanna liked the same kind of movies he did, she'd been his go-to movie companion.

Obviously the next time he was looking for a romantic relationship, he should look for someone more like Susanna.

Or maybe he should actually look at Susanna.

He immediately dismissed that idea out of hand. *Why?*

Because she was *Susanna*. Because they were *friends*. And because the possibility of screwing up his relationship with her wasn't one that he wanted to contemplate.

"You look as if your mind is a hundred miles away," Hutch noted. "Anything you want to talk about?"

Dean snapped his attention back to the present. "I was just thinking how lucky you and Mom are, that—even after forty-five years of marriage—you still enjoy hanging out together."

"Luck has nothing to do with it," Hutch said. "Staying connected requires effort and commitment."

"Is that a commentary on my broken engagement?" he wondered aloud.

"Not at all," his dad said. "Whitney was a lovely girl, but she wasn't right for you."

"You didn't express any concerns when we got engaged," Dean pointed out.

"Because it was your decision to make, and your mom and I always try to support the decisions our children make—even the wrong ones."

He managed to smile at that. "So how will I know when I'm making the right one?"

"You'll know," Hutch said confidently.

Dean might have pursued the topic further, but then his mom called them for dinner.

The food was delicious and conversation interesting throughout the meal, but when the table had been cleared and dishes were done, Dean said a quick goodbye and left his parents to watch *Smokey and the Bandit*—one of their favorite movies and the first one they ever saw together when they were dating.

It was bad enough being a third wheel at the table. He wasn't going to hang around to be a third wheel while they took a romantic walk down memory lane.

But somehow, going home to his empty cabin seemed almost worse.

Susanna went into work early Monday morning to put the finishing touches on the decorating she'd started on the weekend. The first year she'd worked at Abernathy Meats, there had been a tabletop tree on the reception desk—and that was the sum total of the decorations. The following year she asked if she could add a few more holiday touches—some lights to frame the windows and snowflakes to hang from the ceiling. Hannah Abernathy had invited her to "go wild," admitting that she did so much decorating at the Flying A homestead that she didn't have any enthusiasm left to transform the office.

Susanna didn't go wild. Not the first year, anyway. But every year after that, she'd added a little bit more so that now the office looked like a winter wonderland. The focus was Christmas, but Chanukah and Kwanzaa were represented, too.

"Wow, Susanna—you've really outdone yourself this year," Hannah said, turning in a circle to view the decorations around the office.

"Is it too much?" she asked worriedly.

"Too much Christmas?" the older woman scoffed. "I don't think there is such a thing."

"That's how I feel, too," she confided. "But my mom said 'no way' when I brought Sir Kringle home, so now he's here."

"Your mom didn't like him?" Hannah stepped closer to the larger-than-life nutcracker to scrutinize his bright blue uniform with silky red fringe on the epaulettes and gold braid trim on his hat.

"She claimed we don't have room for him, which might be true," Susanna acknowledged. "I've been collecting nutcrackers for a long time and we've got some in every room of the house—even the bathroom."

Hannah smiled at that. "Where did you get Sir Kringle?" she asked.

"At an estate sale."

"I hope you didn't have to wrangle him in here by yourself."

"He comes apart," Susanna said. "But even in three pieces, he's heavy. Luckily, I had Marty to give me a hand."

"That was lucky, but not really surprising. You've been spending a lot of time with your costar lately."

"Every minute I can," she admitted. "He's so talented and experienced, and I'm grateful that he's willing to answer all my questions and help me hone my skills."

"You're not without talent and experience yourself," Hannah said kindly. "For as long as I've known you, you've been involved with the theater."

"High school drama club, college productions and community theater," Susanna noted. "None of which can compare to a New York stage."

"Maybe not, but I have no doubt the Bronco Theater Company is grateful you never took your talents to Broadway."

It was the sincerity in Hannah's tone even more than the words that made Susanna's throat feel tight. "Well, I'm sure Sir Kringle is grateful, anyway," she said. "Because there definitely wouldn't be room for him in a studio walkup in Flatbush."

"He is a very handsome addition to the office," Hannah said.

"Then it's okay if I put him into storage with the rest of your decorations after the holidays?"

"Of course. And speaking of the holidays…what are your plans?"

"The usual," she said. Which meant a quiet meal at home with her mom. And maybe Ted.

Joyce had been hinting that she might invite her friend—she refused to refer to him as her boyfriend, claiming it was a ridiculous label to put on a fifty-five-year-old man—to celebrate with them this year. Susanna had encouraged her to issue the invitation, but her mom wasn't entirely convinced she was ready to take that big a step in their relationship. Perhaps because it had been just Joyce and Susanna for so many years, she was reluctant to change the dynamic. But to Susanna, that was all the more reason to mix things up. And although she'd only met Ted twice, he seemed like a good guy. And he made her mom smile, which Joyce hadn't done often enough before he came into her life.

"You should come to the Flying A on Christmas Eve," Hannah said now. "And bring your mom."

"Actually, my mom's already got plans for Christmas Eve. A secret Santa event hosted by one of her coworkers."

"All the more reason for you to come then," Hannah told her.

"Except that your annual dessert party is a family thing."

"And we consider you a part of the family."

"I know," she said.

And for the most part, she was grateful that it was true. There were times when she even felt as if she was part of the Abernathy family. Certainly Garrett, Dean, Weston, Crosby and Tyler all treated her as if she was their sister. But she didn't want Dean to think of her as a sibling, and it was getting harder and harder to spend time around him and pretend otherwise.

"So you'll come?" Hannah prompted.

Susanna wanted to say yes. Not just because the possibility of seeing Dean was always better than not seeing Dean, but also because she sincerely loved the rest of his family, too. But Winona's cryptic comment about Susanna's heart belonging to another had led her to do some serious soul-searching over the weekend, and she'd realized that seeing Dean almost every day was probably the main reason she hadn't been able to fall for anyone else. And if she was ever going to get over her infatuation with the cowboy, she needed to set boundaries for herself.

But Hannah was still waiting for an answer—and she clearly expected that answer to be yes.

"I'll think about it," Susanna said instead.

And though it was really hard not to immediately change her response when she saw the obvious disappointment on Hannah's face, she didn't do so.

Because, boundaries.

Winona Cobbs sat at her desk with a cup of tea and tried to summon some enthusiasm for her afternoon appointments.

Four women were scheduled to arrive at two o'clock—a bride-to-be and her attendants.

It would be foolish to turn away paying customers, but Winona instinctively knew that none of the women would be sincerely interested in anything she had to tell them. She was just the afternoon's entertainment—more costly than a cineplex matinee but also more uniquely entertaining, something they would giggle over with other friends and family members.

She gave a mental shrug as she sipped her tea.

But why not?

It wasn't as if she had anything better to do with her time.

Her daughter, Dorothea—after almost a year, Winona still got a little thrill out of those words, still marveled over the realization that the baby she'd been told had died at birth was alive and well and now an important part of her life—worried that she was too old to be running a business. But Wisdom by Winona was more of a mission than a business. She had a gift that she wanted to share with the world—for a modest price, of course.

But in an effort to lessen Dorothea's worry, Winona had suggested hanging up her shingle near Bronco Ghost Tours—the business owned and operated by her great-grandson Evan Cruise. She'd started out in a shed behind the main building, and she'd absolutely loved the private space. The turquoise-painted rough plank siding had been decorated with stars and crescent moons, with a Wisdom by Winona sign hung above the purple door.

Unfortunately, the shed wasn't insulated very well—or maybe not at all—and when summer turned to fall and the weather grew colder, Evan had insisted that she move into the main building.

She pulled a flowing purple caftan on over her turquoise turtleneck sweater and jeans, then wrapped a purple turban around her white hair, affixing her favorite crescent moon brooch at the center. Her costume was a little over the top, perhaps, but Winona hadn't earned her eccentric reputation by blending into the background, and she wasn't about to start now.

She selected the desired incense powders—sandalwood to promote a tranquil atmosphere and vanilla to improve mental focus—and dimmed the lights in the waiting area, separated from her consultation chamber by heavy velvet curtains.

She was excited to greet her guests, and perhaps just a tiny bit envious, too, as she thought about the bride-to-be looking forward to a life with the man she loved by her side. Because Winona knew that there was nothing more powerful than first love... and nothing more devastating than its loss.

Susanna was surprised—and pleased—when she got a text message from Callie Sheldrick asking if she was available to meet for coffee.

Half an hour later, she walked into Bronco Java and Juice.

From behind the counter, Cassidy greeted her with a smile and a wave. "Caramel macchiato coming right up."

Though Susanna's mouth was already watering in anticipation of the flavorful treat, she shook her head. "Just a black coffee today, please."

"Well, that's boring," her friend teased. "Who are you and what did you do with the real Susanna Henry?"

"I left her at the theater," she said, making the proprietor laugh.

Callie came in and placed her order as Cassidy was making the boring black coffee, then they paid for their beverages and carried them to a table.

"I know it's a busy time of year for everyone," Callie said. "And even more so for you, with your play opening up in just a few weeks, so I'm glad you were able to squeeze me into your schedule."

"I'm always happy to make time for my friends," Susanna said. "And I've hardly seen you since you got engaged."

A smile curved Callie's lips as she glanced automatically at the diamond winking on her finger. "I've been keeping busy with Tyler and Maeve," she confided. "And packing for my move out to the ranch."

"Exciting times," Susanna said, sincerely happy for her friend.

"While I was going through my desk, I found something." Callie pulled a large envelope out of her purse and passed it across the table.

Her curiosity piqued, Susanna opened the flap and

pulled out the sheaf of papers. The cover page read: *Endings & Beginnings—a play by Susanna Henry.*

"Oh. Wow. I almost forgot that I ever gave this to you," she confided.

When Susanna had written her first play, several years earlier, Callie was one of the few people she'd told. Her friend had been excited for her and eager to read it, and so had become Susanna's first—and so far only—beta reader.

Endings & Beginnings wasn't a play that she ever planned on sharing with anyone, because the story about Annabelle and David was markedly different in tone from her other work. But Callie had been going through a difficult breakup and was desperate for a distraction, so Susanna had offered her the story. Then the ex-boyfriend had come back, at least for a while, and the play had been forgotten—apparently by both of them.

"Well, I finally did read it," Callie said.

"And now I feel compelled to ask you what you thought, though I'm not sure I want to know."

"The writing is really good," her friend assured her. "The characters are realistic and the dialogue is engaging."

"But you didn't love it," she guessed.

"I was just a little disappointed that Annabelle didn't get a happy ending."

"She did, though," Susanna pointed out. "She's starting a new life in a new city, and she's excited about her future."

"A future without David."

She shrugged. "Not everyone gets to be with the person they love."

"But she didn't even try," Callie protested. "You portray Annabelle as this brave woman, venturing off to the big city on her own, but if she was really brave, she'd tell the man she loves the truth about her feelings."

Spoken like a woman in love who was confident that she was loved in return, Susanna mused, though she remained unconvinced.

"Why would she pour out her heart to a man who obviously doesn't love her?" she challenged.

"I don't think that was obvious at all."

"I wrote the play a long time ago—" after she'd learned that Dean and Whitney were engaged "—but I seem to recall that he was planning to marry another woman."

"Plans change," Callie said matter-of-factly. "Take Tyler's brother Dean, for example."

Susanna choked on her coffee. "What about Dean?"

"Tyler told me that he was engaged once—but he and his fiancée never even set a wedding date and everyone in the family breathed a sigh of relief when the engagement was called off."

That was news to Susanna. She'd been certain she was the only one who'd quietly celebrated the end of the engagement, even as she'd worried that Whitney might have broken Dean's heart irreparably.

"Well, the story isn't about Annabelle and Dean," she said. "It's about Annabelle and David."

"And it's a good story," Callie said. "I just wish Annabelle and David had ended up together—like Holly and Noel in *A Christmas Wish*."

"Speaking of happy endings—and beginnings— tell me about your plans for Christmas with Tyler and Maeve."

Callie was only too willing to oblige, and they chatted for another half an hour before Susanna had to head over to the theater for rehearsal.

"Do me a favor?" Callie said as they walked out of the café together.

"Of course," Susanna agreed readily.

"Rewrite Annabelle and David's story and give them a happy ending?"

Though the request wasn't anything that she might have anticipated, she nodded. "I can do that."

Because editing a fictional story was easy; fixing what was wrong in her life was a much more difficult task.

Chapter Four

Like his father and grandfather and great-grandfather before him, Dean was a rancher, which meant that he was more comfortable on horseback than in an office. But raising cattle was a business, and sometimes that business required him to ride a desk rather than his favorite stallion. Though he used to balk at being stuck inside, he'd learned to enjoy the company of people as much as animals. And in the eight years that had passed since she was hired as a part-time receptionist at Abernathy Meats, Susanna Henry had become one of his favorite people.

Even as a teenager, she'd had a way about her that made others feel at ease. She'd also had an unexpected poise and self-confidence that gave clients the impression she was older than her years, and an independent streak that Dean admired even if her determination to do everything on her own exasperated him sometimes. But even more than all that, what he appreciated most about Susanna was the way she looked at him, as if she really saw him. Not just one of Hutch and Hannah's five sons, but *him*. And when she smiled at him, he felt as if the sun was shining, even on the cloudiest days.

"You're not taking lunch today?" Dean asked, when he walked into the office at twelve thirty on Monday and found Susanna at her desk.

"No. I'm working through so that I can take off a little early. Your dad said it's okay," she hastened to assure him.

"Of course it's okay," he said, because he knew that Susanna had always been a diligent employee— and because her hours were really none of his concern, anyway. Just because his name was Abernathy didn't mean that he had any actual say in the running of the business, though he and his brothers had a plan to change that. "Rehearsal tonight?"

"Actually, it's the costume parade tonight."

"I have no idea what that is," he admitted.

"It's exactly what it sounds like," she told him. "We put on our costumes and walk through our scenes, so the costume designer can see how we look under the lights and in specific positions to determine if she needs to tweak anything."

"Like what?"

"Well, aside from the obvious fitting, you want to ensure that the actors don't blend into the setting. For example, there's a scene where we're decorating a Christmas tree, so the costume designer won't want us wearing green."

"When you say 'us,' you mean you and Marty?" he guessed.

"Actually, Avery and Roger are in that scene, too."

"And when does Santa come in?"

"Christmas Eve, of course," she said, her brown eyes sparkling.

How had he never noticed that her eyes were the color of rich dark chocolate?

And why was he noticing now?

Not having a ready answer to either question, he determinedly pushed them to the back of his mind.

"Actually, now that I think about it, you never mentioned who would be playing the jolly old man himself," he said.

She answered without missing a beat: "Kris Kringle."

He rolled his eyes. "I think that's my cue to exit stage left."

"Stage directions are given from the perspective of the actor facing the audience," she told him. "So you'd be exiting stage right."

"Have a good day, Susanna."

"Wait," she said, as he started to turn away.

He waited.

"I've put in for a couple of days off, just before the opening," she said, rifling through the papers on her desk.

"Why are you telling me?"

"Because I sent the request to your dad, via email, as I always do. But you know your dad and email, so I printed a copy." She found what she was looking for, then offered him the page. "If you're on your way to see him, can you drop this on his desk?"

"Sure," he agreed, but his gaze was snagged by a

snap-top container on the corner of her desk that had been revealed by her search for the requisite document. "Are those your sugar cookies?"

"They are," she admitted. "And they're for rehearsal tonight, so hands off."

"But you said it's not a rehearsal, it's..." he paused, trying to remember the term she'd used "...a wardrobe circus."

She rolled her eyes. "Costume parade."

"Right." He smiled winningly.

"We're still going to block some scenes. And it's my turn to supply the snacks tonight."

"It looks like there are a lot of cookies there."

"There are a lot of people needed to put together a production," she told him. "And they're all volunteering their time and talents." But she relented and opened the lid of the container. "You can have *one*."

He grinned and reached inside for a cookie. "Thanks."

"Wipe the crumbs off your shirt before any of your brothers see you. I can't be giving all my cookies away."

"But I got one, because I'm your favorite, right?" he said, with a wink.

Susanna's cheeks turned pink, making him think there might be some truth in his teasing remark. And really, he should be her favorite. Because despite the difference in their ages, they'd become good friends over the years, spending a fair amount of time together outside of work. When she wanted to learn how to ride, he was the one who'd saddled up a gentle mare and shown her the ropes. And when he needed a woman's input on a relationship issue, she was the one he turned to for advice.

Of course, it had been a while since he'd needed her advice, because it had been a while since he'd been in a relationship. And while he generally didn't mind being on his own, recently he'd started to feel as if something important was missing from his life.

Or maybe some*one*.

"Now that you got your cookie, go—" she made a shooing motion with her hand "—so I can get my work done."

He offered a salute and an easy grin. "Yes, ma'am."

But Susanna had already returned her attention to whatever was on her computer.

Dean was cold and hungry when he finally headed back to the barn after fixing a section of downed fence Wednesday morning. Or was it afternoon? He'd been outside for so long, he'd completely lost track of the time. Garrett and Crosby had been out with him, too, but his older brother had already gone back to his cabin for a hot shower, so it was only Crosby with Dean when they rounded the corner of the barn in time to see a vaguely familiar figure climb out of an SUV parked in the visitor lot outside Abernathy Meats.

"What's *he* doing here?" Dean grumbled.

Crosby halted beside him. "Who?"

Dean jerked his head to indicate the man now making his way toward the door that led to the administrative offices.

His brother lifted a hand to shade his eyes. "Is that Marty Trujillo?"

"Yeah."

"Then I'd guess that he's here to see Susanna," Crosby said matter-of-factly.

"Why?"

"They've been running through their lines together on her lunch break."

"You say that as if this isn't the first time he's come here," Dean noted.

"Because it's not," his brother informed him. "He's been here every Wednesday for the past few weeks."

A revelation that did nothing to lighten his suddenly dark mood. "Don't they have rehearsals almost every day after work?"

"Yeah, but you know what a perfectionist Susanna is," Crosby reminded him. "Probably more so than usual with this production, because it's got her name on it."

It was a reasonable explanation, Dean acknowledged.

And yet, he couldn't shake his feeling of unease.

"I'm going to grab a hot shower before we meet in the office to go over our plans for the bison," Crosby said. "It's balls-freezing-below-zero out here and I need to thaw out."

Dean nodded. He should do the same, but he couldn't stop thinking about Susanna in her office with Marty, rehearsing lines together.

Maybe even rehearsing the kiss they'd share on-stage.

Hot coffee, he decided, would be almost as good as a hot shower.

And Susanna had a Keurig and a stock of pods of his favorite dark roast in her office.

He grabbed a mug from the staff kitchen—and gave a fleeting glance to the mostly empty coffee-pot on the warmer there before making his way to her office. He rapped his knuckles on her partially open door, hard enough that it opened a little farther, allowing him to peek inside.

Susanna was standing in front of her desk, fac-ing Marty. Both had copies of what he assumed was the script in their hands. Both glanced over when he poked his head into the room.

"Sorry to interrupt," he lied. "I didn't realize you had company."

"It's okay," Susanna said. "What do you need?"

He held up his empty mug. "Coffee?"

"Did Garrett empty the pot in the kitchen again?"

"There was a tiny bit left." He indicated with his thumb and forefinger. "Not enough for anyone to actually drink."

"Just enough that he could say he didn't finish it," she mused, gesturing to the Keurig on the filing cabinet behind her desk. "Help yourself."

"Thanks."

He selected a pod and popped it into the machine, then set his mug under the spout.

He noted the two mugs on her desk.

"Do either of you want a refill?" he asked.

"No, we're good," Susanna said.

Dean shrugged and picked up his mug. "Well, thanks for the coffee."

"Anytime."

He started toward the door.

"Dean?"

He turned around.

"Can you close that on your way out?"

He wanted to say, *No way in hell*.

But, of course, he had no reason to decline her perfectly reasonable request.

"Oh. Um. Sure," he said instead.

Then he gritted his teeth and closed the door.

"What's going on?" Susanna asked her costar after Dean had gone, leaving them alone again.

Marty feigned ignorance. "What do you mean?"

"You're uncharacteristically unfocused today."

Since he obviously couldn't deny it was true, instead he said, "I'm here to rehearse—not dump my problems on you."

"So there is a problem."

"Yeah, at the end of the second scene, I was thinking that we should—"

She snatched the script out of his hand. "I know

we've only worked together on a couple of productions so far, but I thought, during that time, that we'd become friends."

"We did. We are," he agreed.

"So tell me what's going on."

Marty sighed. "Brian's mom called last night to invite us to celebrate Christmas in Florida with the family."

"I thought his parents lived in Texas."

"Exactly."

"I want to be supportive," Susanna said. "But I'm going to need a little more information."

"His parents rented a four-bedroom house on Belleair Beach so that the family can be together. Never mind that they have a five-bedroom house in Houston, but if we went there for the holidays, it would be hard for my father-in-law to continue pretending to friends and neighbors that his oldest son is straight."

"You've been married for three years and he's still pretending?"

He nodded.

"I'm sorry," Susanna said.

"And Brian was so happy that his parents made an overture, he didn't seem to realize that his dad is still trying to hide us away. And I know I shouldn't judge, but I don't think it's too much to expect him to accept his son for who he is."

"Of course it's not," she agreed.

"Thank you," he said.

"So…have you told Brian that you don't want to go?"

"I didn't say I don't want to go," Marty hedged.

"Maybe not in so many words," she acknowledged. "But I'm pretty good at reading between the lines."

Her costar sighed again. "And you're right—I don't want to go. But not only because they've invited us to Florida instead of Texas, but because it's our first Christmas in our new home, and I was looking forward to actually spending it in our new home."

"So tell Brian that," Susanna urged.

"I was going to, but then I realized that we'll have plenty of other Christmases to spend together in our home," he acknowledged. "Even if none of those will be the first."

Susanna put a gentle hand on her friend's arm and met his gaze. "Talk. To. Your. Husband."

Still, Marty hesitated. "I don't want to create a problem where there isn't one."

"You never know—he might be feeling the same way."

"Maybe," he said dubiously. "But Brian sounded pretty excited about playing golf rather than shoveling snow over the holidays."

"So maybe you could fly down after Christmas and celebrate the New Year on the beach with his family," she suggested.

"That's not a bad idea," he acknowledged.

"Whatever you decide to do, you and Brian should make the decision together."

"You're right."

Susanna huffed out a breath when another knock sounded. "I'm so sorry," she said to Marty. "I hardly ever close my door, but when I do, most people know that it means I don't want to be disturbed."

"There's no reason for you to apologize," he assured her.

"Come in," she called out, with a touch of impatience in her voice now.

Dean poked his head into her office. "More coffee?" he asked, offering her an apologetic smile.

She gestured toward the pods and immediately turned her attention back to Marty, pretending to pick up their conversation where they'd left off. "I know Chuck suggested that we do a set change here, but I was thinking it would simplify things if Noel was coming in as Jack was going out."

"Because if the two men cross paths, then each will know that the other was spending time with Holly," Marty said, not missing a beat.

Susanna nodded. "Exactly."

"I think it's a great idea," he agreed. "Let's talk to Roger before rehearsal tonight and run it that way, to show Chuck how well it works."

Dean took his coffee and walked out, forgetting to close the door again.

With a mutter of frustration, Susanna crossed the room to do so.

"Now, where were we?" she asked.

"Noel coming in as Jack is going out," Marty said.

She shook her head. "That aside was for Dean's benefit."

"It's a good idea, though."

"But we weren't finished talking about your holiday plans."

"But you convinced me to talk to Brian," he told her. "Because I really do like the idea of going to Florida after Christmas."

"Well, that's good, then," she decided.

"And what are your plans for the holidays?"

Before she could respond, another knock sounded on the door.

"I'm busy," she said, directing her remark to whoever was on the other side of the closed door.

Dean, probably assuming that she'd respond with "Come in" again, opened it.

"Which part of 'I'm busy' was unclear?" she asked, exasperated.

The handsome cowboy immediately looked chagrined. "Sorry, but Weston can't find the binder clips."

"Then why isn't Weston knocking on my door?"

"Because he's tearing apart the supply closet, and I thought you'd prefer to find them for us rather than have to put it back together when he's done."

She sighed and dropped her script on her desk, because he was right.

"I'll be right back," she promised Marty.

The other man didn't look annoyed, or even inconvenienced. Instead, Susanna thought that he seemed almost...amused?

She pondered his reaction as she made her way to the supply closet. It took her less than a minute to locate the binder clips Weston apparently wanted, and another five to rearrange the boxes he'd disturbed in his search—which was three minutes longer than she should have needed to complete the simple task, because Dean insisted on trying to help her. But he was more of a hindrance than a help, as he shifted items and peppered her with questions about the organization of the supplies, as if the topic was of great interest to him all of a sudden.

"So...what's your relationship with the cowboy who obviously doesn't like you being alone with another man behind a closed door?" Marty asked, when she finally returned to her office.

"Dean?"

He shrugged.

"I didn't realize you hadn't met," she said. "I should have introduced you."

"Which doesn't answer my question," her costar pointed out.

"We're friends. At least, we used to be," she said. "I'm currently reconsidering that status."

Marty smiled at the obviously empty threat.

"Were you ever something more than friends?" he asked curiously.

Susanna shook her head. "Definitely not."

"That was a pretty emphatic response," he noted.

"I've known Dean for eight years," she explained. "And he's never treated me like anything other than a little sister."

"Hmm."

"What is that supposed to mean?"

"I'm just now realizing that this play we're doing might be more than a little semi-autobiographical."

"It's not," she said quickly.

Perhaps too quickly.

"Because you don't yet have your happy ending?" Marty guessed.

And she was trying to accept that she never would.

Not with Dean, anyway.

"We've probably got time to run through the last scene before you have to head back to school," Susanna said, in an effort to salvage some of their rehearsal time as much as to sidestep his question.

"Or you could tell me how long you've been in love with Dean," her costar suggested.

Unable to avoid Marty's comments any longer, she closed her eyes. "Please tell me I'm not that obvious?"

"You're not that obvious," he intoned dutifully.

"And yet it only took you five minutes to pick up on my feelings," she noted.

"Like you, I have keenly developed observation skills. Your cowboy, on the other hand, is apparently clueless."

"Thank goodness for small favors."

"And sometimes a man needs only to think that another man finds a woman attractive before he actually sees her," Marty continued.

She frowned. "I'm not following."

"I don't think your cowboy is simply protective of you," he said. "I think he's jealous."

Jealous?

Dean?

Susanna immediately shook her head.

"He'd have to be interested in order to feel jealous," she pointed out. "And he knows that the only romance between you and me is on the stage."

"And how does he know that?" her costar asked curiously.

"Because I told him."

"Because he asked?" Marty prompted.

"Yeah," she admitted.

"Because the idea of you and me together obviously bothered him."

"He did comment that you're too old for me," she confided now.

Marty grinned at that. "Did you tell him there were more important reasons that I'm completely wrong for you—such as the fact that I'm married? To a man?" He shook his head without giving her a chance to respond. "Of course you didn't. But it doesn't matter. How old is your cowboy?"

"Stop calling him that. He's not *my* cowboy."

Unfortunately.

Marty waited.

"He's thirty-four," she finally said.

Her costar nodded. "And that's why he's hung up on the age thing—because he thinks that *he's* too old for you."

Susanna sighed. "I wish that was true. But the truth is, Dean doesn't think of me as a potential romantic interest at all but a little sister that he needs to watch out for."

"I'm sure you have reasons for believing that's true, but let me assure you, I saw the way he was looking at you, and there was nothing brotherly about that look."

"What has you all bent out of shape today?" Weston asked, when Dean made his way back to the conference room where his four brothers were waiting to review their plans to bring bison to the ranch.

The idea had first been proposed by their cousin Gabe for the neighboring Ambling A, but immediately rejected by his father, George, who insisted that Abernathys were cattle farmers. George's brother Hutch hadn't exactly embraced the idea, either, but he'd at least agreed to let his sons give it a go, so long as it didn't cost him too much money. The more research Dean and his brothers did, the more convinced they were that Gabe had been onto something—and something that would, in the end, make a lot more money than it cost.

When Dean had given his cousin a heads-up about their plans, Gabe had wished them luck. He wasn't at all upset that they were moving forward with what had originally been his idea. Of course, Gabe had other things to keep him busy—not just an impressive investment portfolio but his beautiful new bride, Melanie.

"Nothing," Dean said now in response to his brother's question.

"Except for the fact that Marty's here again," Crosby countered.

"I should have guessed," Weston realized.

"What are you guys talking about?" Garrett asked, while Dean just scowled.

"That's right—you weren't at the tree lighting," Crosby noted.

"So you didn't see the way Dean was watching Susanna and her costar with a disapproving glower," Weston chimed in.

"Why the disapproval?" Garrett asked.

"I just don't think he's right for her," Dean said.

"What would make him right to play the part of her onstage boyfriend?" his older brother asked.

"I'm sure he's qualified for the onstage part," Dean acknowledged. "I'm more concerned about what's happening offstage."

"You think he has a romantic interest in Susanna?" Crosby asked.

"Why wouldn't he? She's a smart, beautiful woman," Dean noted.

"And apparently our brother Dean is finally realizing that Susanna has a lot to offer," Weston said, sounding amused.

"And that he wants to audition for the role of real-life boyfriend," Crosby added.

"That's ridiculous," Dean protested. "I'm only looking out for Susanna like any brother would look out for his sister."

"Except that you're not my brother and I can take care of myself!"

At the sound of the female voice—a familiar and clearly agitated female voice—Dean spun around.

Standing in the doorway of the conference room was Susanna herself. Glaring at him.

"Uh-oh," Weston muttered under his breath.

"Busted," Tyler agreed.

Dean stood his ground. "You don't exactly have the best track record when it comes to relationships," he pointed out to her.

"Zip it, bro," Crosby urged in a whisper.

"I'm not saying anything that isn't true," Dean insisted.

"Truth doesn't matter," Garrett warned.

Her dark gaze swept over the five Abernathy men. "I'm glad you all find it so entertaining to dissect and analyze my personal life that you can't resist doing so, even in the office."

"Are you saying that you *are* personally involved with Marty?" Dean asked.

"I'm saying that what I do on my own time is my own business," she said coolly.

"Unless you're doing it here," he said.

"He really doesn't know when to shut up, does he?" Weston muttered.

"Totally clueless," Crosby decided.

"About so many things," Tyler agreed.

Susanna ignored them. "We've been rehearsing in my office because Marty has a free period before lunch, which means that he has time to drive here and back and run lines with me for almost a full hour. But if it's a problem, I can meet him at the school— or maybe his place would be more convenient, since it's about halfway between here and there."

"It's not a problem," Dean was quick to assure her.

"Maybe not for you," she said. "But the interruptions are a problem for me."

"I'm sorry," he said, sincerely contrite. "I promise it won't happen again."

"And I promise to consider forgiving you, but it's not going to happen today," she retorted.

Then, with her head held high, Susanna turned and exited stage right, leaving Dean with the uncomfortable realization that he'd hurt his friend—and with his four brothers who were still talking about the fact that *he* didn't know when to shut up.

Chapter Five

The costume parade was a disaster—if only from Susanna's perspective. Then again, she'd anticipated that there might be some friction when she discovered that Irene Krecji—mother of Alicia of "The Dorothy Setback"—had signed on as the costume designer.

More than a decade had passed since Susanna was passed over for the role of Dorothy, and though Irene had preened in the wings at every rehearsal as her daughter followed the yellow brick road, she'd yet to get over what happened on opening night. Alicia had done a great job preparing for the show: she'd memorized all her lines and knew how to take direction. But although she was pretty and popular and had no trouble holding court with her clique, she was always nervous whenever she had to present in front of the whole class.

So when Alicia peeked out from behind the curtain on opening night and saw there wasn't an empty seat in the gymnatorium, she panicked. And then she threw up, and she couldn't stop throwing up. Irene had been adamant that her daughter just needed a minute and then she'd be ready to go on and be the star of the show.

Because she *was* the star—she was *Dorothy*, Irene kept insisting, even while Miss Fitzgerald was helping Susanna squeeze into Dorothy's gingham pinafore and Hardik Rattan was plucked from the Lollipop Guild to take over the role of the cowardly lion.

Afterward, Susanna overheard Alicia's boyfriend joke, in an effort to make the sidelined star of the show feel better, that it wasn't Dorothy's house that killed the Wicked Witch of the East, but the weight of Susanna-as-Dorothy in the house when it came down on top of her.

Susanna refused to let his snide remark bother her, because she knew that she'd saved the show. And so did Irene Krecji, who'd apparently never forgiven her for upstaging her daughter—never mind that Alicia had been clinging to a bucket right up until Dorothy had clicked her heels together three times.

"I didn't realize anyone else was still here," Susanna said, when she walked into the kitchenette to retrieve her cookie container and found Avery Lang, one of the actors, seated at the small bistro-style table. "You're usually the first one out the door on Wednesdays."

"Because I have an early class on Thursdays," Avery said. "Which finished last week. My final exam is Saturday morning."

"I don't know how you juggle school, work and the play."

"I took a break from the theater for a couple years, because I wasn't sure I could manage—and I was right," Avery confided wearily.

"I can't comment on your performance in the classroom or at your job, but you've done a fabulous job bringing Joy to life," Susanna told her.

"I like her," Avery said. "Which makes it not just easy but fun to get into character. And her friendship with Holly is so relatable and real."

"I'm glad you think so."

"And I know that you and I don't have the same history as Holly and Joy, and maybe I'm overstepping by saying anything, but it needs to be said— Irene is a world-class bitch."

"You heard her talking to me about my costume," Susanna realized, surprised by the fierceness of the other woman's tone.

"She didn't make any effort to keep her voice down."

Susanna winced. "So I should assume everyone heard what she said?"

"No, just me," Avery said. "The others had already skipped out to ensure they got their share of cookies."

"I guess I should be grateful for that, then."

"I almost wish Chuck had heard her. I can't imagine he would have stayed silent." Avery shook her head. "She put you in a dress that's a size too small and then told you it would fit better if you lost a few pounds."

"Irene's never made any secret of the fact that she believes I should be backstage rather than onstage."

"I gather the two of you have a history," Avery said.

"I went to school with her daughter," Susanna explained. "Alicia and I often competed for the same roles."

"And she didn't like that you always won them," Avery guessed.

"Actually, Alicia won more often than I did."

After Irene took her daughter to a psychologist to help her conquer her debilitating stage fright and hired a private drama coach to ensure she was primed for every one of her auditions.

To provide her castmate with context, Susanna quickly recapped the story about *The Wizard of Oz* production.

"So she's been holding a grudge since you were in middle school?" Avery was incredulous.

Susanna just shrugged. "She was convinced that her daughter was a star."

"Where is Alicia now?"

"Last I heard, she was in LA."

Avery's brows lifted. "Working as an actor?"

"As a stylist in an upscale boutique, but dating an actor from *NCIS: Los Angeles*."

Avery snorted. "Speaking of dating… I've noticed that Roger sticks pretty close to you during rehearsals. Is there anything going on between the two of you?"

"Nothing at all," Susanna told her. Then, because her curiosity was piqued by the question, she couldn't resist asking, "Why? Are you interested?"

"No, but Liz is, and she didn't want to make a move if she'd be stepping on any toes."

"Definitely no toes in danger."

"That was pretty emphatic," the other woman noted. "Is there something you know about him that Liz should know?"

"No, he's a great guy," Susanna hastened to assure her. "I guess I'm just drawn to guys who are a little more mature," she added, thinking—as she always seemed to be—of Dean.

"Or maybe one specific guy?" Avery guessed.

Susanna felt her cheeks flush, but the closest she was willing to come to a confession was to say, "Maybe."

Dean didn't need his brothers to tell him that he'd acted like an ass with Susanna, though of course they were happy to do so. And while he was fairly confident that she would forgive him—he'd never known her to hold a grudge—he decided that a bribe might help him get back into her good graces sooner rather than later.

He gave her a wide berth on Thursday, allowing her some time to cool off, and most of Friday, too, only approaching her office near the end of the day.

She glanced up at the knock on her door, and the smile that lit her face when she saw him told him that he was already forgiven. Or mostly, he amended, when she deliberately straightened her lips again, as if suddenly remembering that she was supposed to be mad at him.

"I brought you a present," he said, setting the box on her desk.

"A present or a peace offering?"

He shrugged. "You can call it whatever you want."

She lifted the lid to peer into the box. "Coffee pods?"

"For your Keurig," he explained.

"Coincidentally, your favorite blend."

"Doesn't everyone like dark roast?"

Susanna moved the box to the side. "Thank you."

He tucked his hands in the front pockets of his jeans. "Are you still mad?"

"No," she said. "I'm not still mad."

"I wasn't sure, because you seemed to be even busier than usual when I came into the office this morning, and I didn't know if you were really busy or just pretending to be busy to avoid talking to me."

"I was—and am—really busy," she assured him. "In case you haven't looked at a calendar, there are only twenty-two days until Christmas and twelve days until opening night of the play."

"I have looked at a calendar," he said. "Which is why I was hoping you might have some free time to help me finish my Christmas shopping."

Dean didn't anticipate a refusal.

To the best of his recollection, Susanna had never turned him down when he asked a favor, but he did wonder if she'd have to check with Marty before agreeing to his request. It seemed as if every free minute she had lately was spent with Marty, and even when she wasn't with her costar, she was talking about him. (According to Crosby, Roger had grumbled about the exact same thing.)

She'd been involved with the theater for as long as he'd known her, but Dean didn't think she'd dated another actor after her breakup with Scott. And despite her insistence that she and Marty were just friends, Susanna seemed to have a real connection with the man, and she was always smiling or laughing when she was in his company.

But Dean had an advantage in that he knew she loved everything about Christmas, so he felt certain that she'd be eager to visit the stores all decked out for the holidays.

But instead of responding to his question with an enthusiastic "yes," she said, "When?"

"What works for you?" he asked, demonstrating his willingness to be flexible.

She opened the calendar app on her phone and scrolled through the days. "I'm pretty busy with rehearsals."

"Even on weekends?" he pressed.

"*Especially* on weekends," she said. "But Chuck's son has a basketball game tomorrow morning, so we're not starting until three, if you want to go shopping for a few hours in the morning."

"Great," he said. "I'll pick you up at eight."

"Isn't that a little early considering that most of the shops don't open until ten?"

"The mall in Rocky Falls opens at nine," he said.

"The mall?" She made a face.

"What's wrong with the mall?"

"Nothing, really," she said. "I just prefer to buy at the local shops rather than trekking to a nearby town."

"Usually I do, too," he told her. "But it takes twice as long to get anything done in Bronco, because every way you turn, you're running into someone you know."

"You obviously know more people than I do," she mused.

"Probably more people know me," he acknowledged. "Or at least my family." Because it was an undeniable fact that the Abernathys and Taylors and Daltons, as the biggest ranching families in town, were treated with something akin to celebrity status in Bronco.

"I guess I'll see you at eight, then," Susanna said.

"Do you have any plans tonight?" he asked, as she began to tidy up her desk in preparation for leaving.

"Rehearsal."

Because she had rehearsal every night.

"But you have to eat, right? So maybe we could go somewhere and grab a bite. Together."

It wasn't an unusual request. Over the years, they'd shared more than a few meals. But she was looking at him now as if his hat had suddenly sprouted horns.

And why wouldn't she be wary?

Because it sounded an awful lot like he was asking her out. And doing an awful job of it.

"I don't mean like a date," he said. Because apparently he couldn't stop talking and making the conversation even more awkward. "Just, you know, two friends grabbing a bite."

"Thanks," she said. "But I've already got plans."

"Oh. Okay."

"With my mom," she clarified.

He was ridiculously relieved to know that she wasn't having dinner with Marty. Or Roger.

Which was a very good reason to end this conversation now and say goodbye to Susanna—at least until tomorrow.

"Great job, people," Chuck said. "Let's do it again tomorrow."

"Great job?" Roger muttered under his breath as the director walked off. "He made me walk out and reenter the set seventeen times."

"It was seven," Susanna said, though not without some sympathy.

Chuck had put them all through their paces tonight, but in the end, he'd been pleased, and when a director of his caliber was pleased, the actors could feel confident that they'd done a good job.

"Still," Roger said. "I think I've earned pizza. You up for a slice?"

"Me?" Susanna asked, surprised.

Roger grinned as he looked around, making her realize there was no one else in the immediate vicinity that he'd be asking.

"Um, pizza sounds great, but I'm going to head home. I've got an early day tomorrow."

"Not here, though, right?" Roger asked.

"Not here," she confirmed. "Rehearsal doesn't start until three tomorrow."

"Which means walking through the door no later than two forty-five," he said, dropping his voice an octave. "Because if you're not early you're late."

Susanna smiled at his surprisingly accurate imitation of the director. "I'll see you at two forty-five tomorrow."

"I'm already looking forward to it," Roger said, and with a quick wave, he was gone.

Susanna picked up the sweater she'd discarded earlier and tugged it over her head.

"I didn't imagine that anyone could own more Christmas sweaters than my mom," Marty commented, making his way toward her and offering her the water bottle she'd left onstage. "Until I met you."

"This one is more wintry than Christmassy," she pointed out, glancing down at the trio of snowmen wearing woolly hats and scarves.

"Still," he said. "We've been rehearsing almost

every day for two weeks, and I don't think I've seen you wear the same sweater twice."

"You will," she said. "Because I've only got twelve."

"Only?"

She shrugged. "I collect Christmas sweaters and nutcrackers."

"Do you have a nutcracker Christmas sweater?"

She grinned. "I'll be wearing that one tomorrow."

"So what had you looking so bemused when Roger left?" her costar asked now.

"A second unexpected invitation to grab a bite to eat."

"Obviously Roger's was the second," he mused. "Who issued the first?"

"Dean."

"Your cowboy finally stepped up and asked you on a date?"

"No," she said quickly. "He was clear that it wouldn't be a date. But still, it was…weird. He was acting weird."

"He's flustered," Marty said. "Trying to figure out why he's suddenly thinking about good old Susanna in ways he's never thought about her before."

She wished she could believe it was true, but she'd been wishing for eight years already.

"Or maybe I'm reading too much into a simple invitation," she decided. "In any event, I told him that I was going home for dinner and that was that."

"Except that now you're going to be thinking

about the invitation—and wondering if you should have said yes—until you see him again on Monday."

"Actually, I'm seeing him tomorrow."

"Do tell," Marty urged.

"It's nothing to get excited about," she assured him. "We're just going Christmas shopping."

"His idea?" he guessed.

She nodded.

"I'm telling you, the man is coming around and finally starting to see the beautiful woman who's been standing in front of him for eight years."

"More likely the man is coming around to see that Christmas is only three weeks away."

He shook his head. "And you're supposed to be a romantic."

"My romanticism has been tempered by reality," she told him. "I've spent too many years already hoping and wishing for something that will never happen."

"Never say never," Marty cautioned.

While Susanna appreciated the wisdom of the sentiment, she'd held on to her fantasies for too long already.

It was time to get over her hopeless infatuation and move on.

Chapter Six

Dean was at Susanna's house by 8:00 a.m. Saturday morning, as promised, and they were parked in a prime spot at the shopping mall in Rocky Falls thirty-five minutes later.

"Which means that we have time for coffee before the stores open," Dean said, holding the door for Susanna.

"Coffee sounds good," she agreed.

Of course, most everyone else who'd decided to get an early start on their shopping had the same idea, and there was a line of customers ahead of them when they entered the coffeehouse.

"They've got holiday specials," Dean said, reading the board. "A chestnut praline frappé, a gingerbread macchiato, an eggnog latte and a peppermint mocha."

"Just regular coffee for me," she said.

"Regular coffee is fine for January through November," he said. "But the holidays warrant a festive indulgence, don't you think?"

She thought that Dean could indulge in whatever he wanted. But she had to be onstage, under bright lights in less than two weeks, so her indulgences would have to wait until Christmas Eve.

"I'm going to try an eggnog latte—and a cranberry-orange scone," Dean decided as he stepped up to the cash register.

"Just regular coffee," Susanna said again, speaking this time to the barista whose name tag identified him as Pietro. "Large. Black."

"Did you want something to eat with that? A batch of soft molasses cookies just came out of the oven."

"No." She forced a smile. "Thank you."

"How can you say no to warm cookies?" Dean asked, sounding appalled. To Pietro he said, "I'll take two of them."

"Instead of the scone?"

"In addition to the scone," he clarified.

The barista happily added the additional items to the order, and Dean tapped his debit card to pay.

They found an empty table and sat down to drink their coffee.

"Since when do you drink your coffee black?" Dean asked, as she took a tentative sip.

"Since I have to be onstage in front of a hopefully packed house in eleven days."

"I don't understand."

Of course, he didn't. Because he was a man—a rancher—with a lean, muscular build, and she was more curvy than was fashionable. And it didn't help that the costume designer had found the perfect dress for Holly in wardrobe—perfect except for the fact that it was a size too small.

Irene had considered letting out the seams, but— as she explained to Susanna—there wasn't a lot of excess material. The implication being, of course, that Susanna needed a lot of excess material. And so she'd advised Susanna to avoid eating too many of the cookies she was always bringing to rehearsal. And maybe invest in a treadmill.

Because Avery was right—Irene Krecji was a bitch.

Instead of trying to explain her weight issues to Dean, she said, "It doesn't matter," and lifted her mug to take another sip of her coffee.

Dean broke off a piece of the cookie and popped it into his mouth. "Mmm...you have to try this," he told her, holding the cookie toward her.

She shook her head. "I can't."

"I don't want to hear any nonsense about you having to be onstage. You'll look hot because you always look hot," he said, proving that he was more insightful than she'd given him credit for being.

And though she was flattered by his words—and more than a little surprised, because she honestly didn't think Dean ever paid any attention to how she looked and certainly wouldn't have anticipated that he'd use the word *hot* to describe her (unless it was because she was sweating under the lights)— she shook her head again. "I really can't."

"One little bite," he urged.

Because he didn't understand that carbs were her enemy and one little bite would make her want another bite—and then another whole cookie.

But she recognized the dog-with-a-bone look in his eye and offered an argument he couldn't refute: "I really can't. I'm allergic to molasses."

He immediately pulled the cookie back, as if he was afraid she might break out in hives because of its proximity. "I'm sorry. I didn't know."

And he was so contrite, she felt just a tiny bit guilty for the lie. "It's okay."

"You want the cranberry scone?"

She shook her head. "I'm not a fan of cranberries."

And that, at least, was the truth.

While Dean polished off the cookies, Susanna retrieved a pen and small notebook from her purse, opened the cover and flipped through the pages until she found a blank one.

"Who do you still have to buy for?" she asked, wanting to make a list to ensure no one was forgotten. But mostly wanting to change the subject.

"My mom and dad. Grandpa. Garrett, Weston, Crosby and Tyler. And Maeve." Thinking of his thirteen-month-old niece, he smiled. "We definitely can't forget Maeve."

She scribbled the names, then looked up at him.

"You haven't done any shopping yet," she realized.

"Why are you surprised?"

"I shouldn't be," she acknowledged. "Except that

it's the fourth of December, so I expected you would have at least started."

"I've been busy."

"Busy procrastinating," she guessed.

He grinned. "You know me so well."

"Plus, you said you wanted some help to *finish* your shopping," she reminded him.

"I'm hoping we can both start and finish today," he said with a wink.

She glanced at her watch. "Then you better hurry up and eat your scone so we can get started."

"We've still got a few minutes until the stores open," he reminded her.

She swallowed another mouthful of coffee and tried not to grimace at the harshness of the flavor undisguised by cream and sugar—or a shot of caramel syrup and whipped cream—as she looked at his list again.

At least this year he wasn't dating anyone, so she wouldn't be expected to help him pick out a gift for his girlfriend.

Then again, he tended to keep his private life private, so she couldn't really be 100 percent certain that he wasn't seeing someone.

"Is this list complete?" she asked.

"You know all my family—is there someone I've missed?"

"Your family is covered," she acknowledged. "I just wondered if there was anyone else, who's not family, that you needed to buy a gift for."

"Well, yeah," he said. "But even I'm not so pathetic that I'm going to buy your Christmas present while you're with me."

"I didn't mean me," she protested. "And you know you don't have to buy me anything."

"I know, but I actually like shopping for you."

And he usually picked up something thoughtful and meaningful. A book of plays by her favorite playwright; a bottle of perfume that she'd admired when they were shopping together—not because she liked the scent as much as she liked the bottle; a Buddy the Elf nutcracker to add to her collection; a pair of fleece-lined mittens because she grumbled that her hands were always cold. And one year he'd stunned her with a beautiful glass pendant that she'd paused to admire in the window of a jewelry store, despite the fact that she hadn't drawn his attention to it in any way.

Thinking about it now, she realized that he paid more attention to the things she said and did than she'd realized. It made her wonder if—and hope that—his thoughtfulness was sparked by affection. But she immediately shook off the possibility, acknowledging that all the Abernathys were kind and considerate, and that his efforts were no doubt a result of his upbringing and not specific to her at all.

"I meant a special someone," she said to him now.

"You don't think you're special?" he asked teasingly.

She huffed out a breath, wondering how it was

that he managed to simultaneously flatter and annoy her.

"Is there a girlfriend you should be shopping for?" she asked bluntly.

"No." He shook his head. Then, "Hmm…maybe that's why my credit card bill didn't almost give me a heart attack last January—because I didn't have a girlfriend last Christmas, either."

"Weren't you dating Bianca last Christmas?"

"No, we didn't hook up—" he cut himself off and faked a cough "—we didn't *meet* until New Year's Eve."

Susanna rolled her eyes. "Did you think I'd be shocked to learn that you hooked up with a woman? Because I'd be willing to bet that Bianca wasn't the first."

"The point is, I wasn't dating anyone last Christmas," he said. "This is the second year in a row that I've been solo during the holidays."

"It's my fourth," Susanna admitted. "But who's counting?"

"It sounds like you are," Dean noted.

She shrugged. "It doesn't bother me to be alone during the holidays—I mean, it shouldn't be any different than any other time of the year, except that there are always more get-togethers with friends, and with every season that passes, more and more of my friends have significant others in their lives, which seems to emphasize my aloneness. And that's even

before they ask, as they inevitably do, 'Are you seeing anyone these days?'"

"And it's never your single friends who ask the
questions, is it?" Dean asked. "It's always the ones
who are married or engaged or in a serious relationship, and there's always a hint of pity in their tone."

"Do guys do the same thing?"

He nodded. "I grabbed a drink with my cousin
Gabe at The Association last week," he said, naming Bronco's private and very exclusive cattleman's
club. "And I'm happy that he's happy, but we couldn't
talk about anything for more than two minutes without Mel's name somehow coming up in the conversation."

"They're newlyweds," Susanna reminded him.

"I know. And I didn't really mind when he went
on and on about how amazing his wife is and how
the sky is bluer and the grass is greener—albeit buried under a couple feet of snow right now."

"Whiter snow?" she teased.

He chuckled. "So much whiter." His expression
sobered again. "Then the topic shifted to Gabe wishing that I might one day find a woman who changes
my life the way Mel changed his. Because yeah, the
bachelor lifestyle might seem great, but it's only
when you find a true partner to share your life that
you realize how empty and lonely it really is."

"How fast did you finish your drink?" she wondered.

"Obviously not fast enough," Dean told her. "And

I don't necessarily disagree with anything he said—I just didn't particularly want to have his marital bliss rubbed in my face.

"Because it's not that I don't want to meet someone," he continued. "But dating just isn't as much fun as it used to be."

"Why is that?" she asked curiously.

"Heck if I know," he said. "Maybe there's a secret switch that gets flipped on your thirtieth birthday. In your twenties, it's okay to go out and have a good time and not want anything more than that. But once you hit the big three-oh—which I know you don't have to worry about for several more years—it's like dating needs to have a purpose, and now I'm supposed to be looking for a woman to marry and have a family with."

"Is that why you proposed to Whitney—because it was what everyone expected?"

"No, we got engaged because it was what Whitney expected," he said. "And we got along well enough that I didn't see any reason to object."

"You're such a romantic," she said dryly.

"Of course I want to get married and have a family someday," he said. "I just don't want to rush down that path."

"Like Garrett and Tyler did," she guessed.

"Yeah," he admitted.

His oldest brother had tied the knot right out of college—and spent the next several years in an unhappy marriage before he and his wife decided to cut their losses and go their separate ways. His younger brother had made a similarly early trip to the altar, but was now a widowed single dad of a baby girl.

And although Tyler was engaged again—and obviously head over heels in love with Callie—it was evident to Susanna that Dean remained wary of giving his heart too readily.

"I'm not in any way trying to downplay the significance of the loss Tyler suffered," Susanna said, "but his marriage resulted in a beautiful baby girl who is the light of his life."

"We all adore Maeve," Dean said.

"Who wouldn't? She's adorable."

"But it was harder for Ty to grieve, I think, while also trying to care for a baby."

"And now he's got Callie by his side."

"Yeah," Dean agreed, though he didn't sound very convinced.

"Do you disapprove of his relationship with Callie?" she asked, prepared to jump to the defense of her friend.

"No," he immediately replied. "I think she's great. And she's great for Ty and Maeve. I just marvel over the fact that my youngest brother is still only twenty-eight years old and making plans to get married for the second time."

Reassured by his response, she teasingly asked, "Do you feel as if you have some catching up to do?"

"No," Dean said again. "The reason Whitney and I broke up is that I only want to get married once, and when I thought about my future…I just couldn't see her there with me."

"Then you obviously made the right choice."

He nodded. "I guess I just wonder sometimes…if I was wrong in believing that I was in love with Whitney, is it possible that I've also been wrong about some of the other women I dated? And will I know the right woman *is* the right woman when I finally meet her?"

You already have, Susanna wanted to tell him. *Just look across the table—she's sitting right here.*

But, of course, she didn't.

"An interesting question," she mused instead. "And one that requires far more contemplation than we have time for now, because it's nine o'clock."

Dean pushed back his chair. "Let's go shopping."

Three and a half hours later, as Dean handed his credit card to the clerk, Susanna checked the last name off his shopping list.

"And you're done," she said, dropping the notebook into the side pocket of her purse.

"Shopping is always so much easier with you," he said.

"You're just saying that because you don't like to shop alone."

Truthfully, he didn't really like shopping at all. Probably because he had so many memories of being dragged around to fancy boutiques by his former fiancée, who loved to shop—and try on clothes—

while his only responsibilities were to tell her how fabulous she looked and carry her purchases.

And she usually did look fabulous. Whitney was one of those women who would look good wearing a potato sack. Not that she ever would, unless the potato sack boasted a designer label and a price tag to match. And then she'd accessorize it with shiny baubles and skyscraper heels.

In retrospect, he didn't know what he'd been thinking when he'd put a ring on her finger. Aside from some impressive chemistry, they really didn't have a lot in common. Whitney liked to go out—to see and be seen—while Dean usually preferred quiet nights at home.

But relationships were about compromise, he'd remind himself as he got ready to go out for dinner with friends who were just back from their honeymoon, or dancing at a club to celebrate the engagement of another couple. However, the more time they spent with Whitney's just-married or soon-to-be-married or practically engaged friends, the clearer it became to Dean that she expected him to put a ring on her finger—and was growing increasingly impatient with waiting. He put it off as long as he could, but when her hints became more obvious than subtle, he could no longer pretend to be oblivious.

Because what was he waiting for?

Didn't he want to get married and start a family, too?

Of course he did—so why was he hesitating?

The answer to that question was apparent to him every time he was with his parents.

He was hesitating because he wanted the kind of relationship that his mom and dad had. He wanted to be with someone who knew him inside and out and loved him anyway. Someone who let him see what was inside her—the good, the bad and the ugly—and trust that he'd love her anyway. And he had doubts about whether Whitney was that woman.

When she said that she loved him, he suspected that she was more in love with the man she wanted him to be than with the man he actually was. And when he said that he loved her, he knew that he didn't want to spend the rest of his life trying to live up to her ideals.

Susanna nudged him with her shoulder, drawing his attention back to the present.

"Sorry," he said. "My mind just wandered for a minute."

"Low blood sugar?" she teased.

"Probably. Hunting down the perfect gifts is hard work."

"Well, I think we've got time for lunch before we head back to Bronco," she said.

"If we go for lunch, are you actually going to eat lunch?"

"I am," she confirmed.

And she did—if a garden salad with light dressing counted as lunch.

He had a teriyaki steak sub with onions and peppers and cheese and a side of potato wedges.

But they chatted easily while they ate, and Dean was reminded again how much he always enjoyed her company—and how little of it he'd had since rehearsals had started for the Christmas play.

"I'm glad it was a successful day for you," Susanna said, as they headed back to his truck after lunch.

"It has been," he agreed. "Though I can't help but notice that all the bags you're carrying are mine."

"Because my shopping is already done."

"I should have guessed. No doubt your gifts are all wrapped, too."

"I only wish," she said.

His surprise wasn't entirely feigned.

She shrugged. "The shopping I did here and there, a little bit at a time. But wrapping is a big job, and I haven't had time to haul out the paper and bows to tackle it just yet."

"Unwrapping is always more fun than wrapping, isn't it?"

"I actually like wrapping. Taking a plain box and dressing it up is fun. To me, anyway," she amended, when he rolled his eyes.

"In that case..." he began.

Susanna immediately shook her head. "No."

"You don't even know what I was going to say," Dean protested.

"Yes, I do," she insisted. "Because I know you,

and I did most of your wrapping last year and the year before that and probably the year before that."

"Probably," he agreed.

"This year, you're on your own."

"But wrapping is another one of those tasks that's a lot more fun if you've got someone to do it with."

"You've got four brothers—pick one of them."

"And with someone who doesn't mind showing you, for the umpteenth time, how to fold the ends so it doesn't look like a second grader wrapped it," he continued, pointedly ignoring her suggestion.

Susanna sighed. "I'd love to help but—"

"Great!" he interjected.

"*But*," she said again, loudly and firmly, "I really am going to be swamped for the next couple of weeks."

"I understand," he said, though he didn't even attempt to hide his obvious disappointment.

And she felt herself wavering.

She hated to say no to him, because it wasn't very often that he asked her for a favor. And because she'd been trying, for more than eight years now, to demonstrate that she was invaluable to him. Believing that if she could make him see that he needed her, then maybe he'd eventually realize that he wanted her, too.

So far, to no avail.

And yet, when she opened her mouth again, she heard herself say, "But I guess I could give you a hand with your gifts, if you want."

"I know I'm taking advantage," he acknowledged. "But you really are a lot better at wrapping than I am."

"Only because you haven't had enough practice," she told him.

"Just tell me when you want to do it, and I'll be there."

"I'll let you know," she promised.

He gave her a quick hug. "Thank you."

As Susanna breathed in his scent, she wondered how it was possible that they'd been walking around the mall for hours but he still smelled like the outdoors—a combination of fresh air with a hint of cedar and something else that was uniquely Dean and dangerously intoxicating.

She wished she could stay in his arms, breathing in that heady scent, forever.

But, of course, she couldn't.

Because she didn't belong with Dean.

Not even for a moment.

And reminding herself of that fact, she eased away from him.

"We should head back so I'm not late for rehearsal."

Chapter Seven

They left the mall in plenty of time for Dean to drop Susanna back at her mom's house to pick up her own car and drive to rehearsal. Plenty of time, that is, if they hadn't got stuck in traffic as the result of a multivehicle collision.

Susanna glanced at her watch for the tenth time in as many minutes as he inched along the highway. "When we get back to Bronco, do you think you could drop me off at the theater instead of taking me home?"

"Of course," he immediately agreed. "And I'll pick you up again when rehearsal is over."

"That's not necessary," she said. "I'm sure Roger won't mind giving me a ride."

"I don't mind, either," Dean said. "In fact, I insist, since it's my fault we're behind schedule."

"It's nobody's fault," she denied. "And I can find my own way home."

"Text me when you're done," he said, in a tone that brooked no argument. "And I'll pick you up."

"You just want to make sure that I take your Christmas gifts home with me to wrap, don't you?" she teased.

He winked. "You know me so well."

"It might be late," Susanna warned. "Chuck doesn't pay much attention to the clock at the best of times—and not at all on Saturdays, and I know you have to be up early in the morning."

"Usually," he agreed. "But one of my brothers will cover my chores if I'm running a little behind schedule in the morning."

As he'd no doubt covered for them in the past, she realized, and nodded.

"All right, then," she agreed. "I'll text you when we're done."

It was almost ten o'clock when Susanna texted to inform Dean that rehearsal was finished, but he was already in the parking lot outside the theater to ensure that he wouldn't keep her waiting. At least that was the rationale he'd given to himself while he huddled in his cold-and-growing-ever-colder vehicle, waiting for her message, periodically starting the engine to crank the heater and defrost the windshield.

He'd passed the time listening to the radio and thinking about his outing with Susanna earlier in the day. He really did *not* like shopping—especially in the midst of holiday crowds—but he'd genuinely enjoyed shopping with Susanna. Of course, he always enjoyed being with her—whether they were in the lunch room at Abernathy Meats or on horseback at the Flying A or at the local movie theater. No doubt, wrapping presents with Susanna would be fun, too, and he was already looking forward to tackling the task with her.

He also liked that he could talk to her about almost anything, and he appreciated her ability to make him laugh even when he was certain he wasn't in the mood to do so. But he wasn't laughing when he saw her walk out of the theater with Roger—after Marty and Avery and Liz were already gone—and he realized that the actor's romantic interest in her was one of the reasons he'd been staked out waiting.

They paused for a moment on the back step, and he guessed that Roger must have asked if she needed a ride, because she shook her head and pointed toward Dean's truck. Crosby's friend then said something else and got another headshake in response. Then he leaned in…

Dean found himself leaning forward, trying to focus on them through the partially fogged window.

Was Roger whispering in her ear?

Or maybe touching his lips to her cheek?

He tapped the horn and stuck his arm out the window to wave, as if to let her know that he was there.

Susanna waved back, and he started the engine and cranked up the heat as she made her way toward his truck.

"Thanks again for coming to get me," Susanna said, as she buckled her seat belt.

"Not a problem." His voice sounded tight, even to

his own ears, and he kept his eyes focused straight ahead.

"Are you sure?" she asked. "Because you sound a little...annoyed."

"I'm just tired," he said. "It's been a long day."

"Which is exactly why I said that I could get a ride with Roger," she pointed out to him.

"Would you have preferred to get a ride with Roger?"

"I was thinking more of practicalities than preferences," she told him. "He drives right past my street on his way home."

No doubt it would have been Roger's preference to take her home—to prolong the time he got to spend in her company.

"Did he kiss you?"

"What?"

She turned to face him, clearly startled—and maybe baffled—by the question he hadn't intended to ask.

"When you were standing on the step outside the theater," he said. "I saw him lean close and...it almost looked like he kissed you."

She shook her head. "Roger and I are *friends*."

He should have been satisfied by that response, because he and Susanna were friends, too. But for some inexplicable reason, her friendship with the other man made him uneasy.

Or maybe the reason wasn't so inexplicable.

...apparently our brother Dean is finally realizing that Susanna has a lot to offer.

Out of nowhere, he heard Weston's words in his head.

And that he wants to audition for the role of real-life boyfriend.

Now it was Crosby's voice that seemed to echo in his mind.

Ridiculous, Dean protested now as he did then, though only to himself this time.

And as much as he wanted to believe that he was looking out for Susanna like any brother would look out for his sister, he'd recently had some thoughts about Susanna that wouldn't be at all appropriate if they were actually siblings.

Because she *was* a smart, beautiful woman, and he was just a man who, like most other men, was easily brought to his knees by a smart, beautiful woman.

And didn't that put an image in his head?

A tantalizing, tempting and wrong-in-so-many-ways image.

Was Crosby right?

Did Dean want more than just friendship from Susanna?

Even if he did, what he wanted was irrelevant. Because she wasn't just a friend, she was nine years younger than him and also an employee of Abernathy Meats. And those were three very good reasons that he couldn't ever make a move on her.

Three very good reasons that nevertheless failed

to stop him from wondering what it would be like to hold her and kiss her…and wanting to find out.

"Sometimes friendship can lead to more," he pointed out.

"One can only hope," she replied.

He frowned at that. "I just think you need to be careful that you're not sending him the wrong signals."

"I'm not sending him the wrong signals," she promised. "I'm not sending him *any* signals."

"You might not think so, but theater people…"

"Please," she said dryly, when his words trailed off. "Tell me what you think you know about theater people."

"Actually, I think I should shut up now."

"That's a good idea," she agreed.

He drove for half a minute in silence, then turned onto Cottonwood Crescent.

"When I said 'theater people,' I didn't mean you," he said.

"I thought you were shutting up."

"I'm trying to explain."

"That's not necessary," she told him.

"I just don't like the way the guy hovers around you," he said, an uncomfortable admission.

"Roger is a fellow cast member," she reminded him. "And a friend. And why do you even care if he hovers or kisses me or if we have sex in the orchestra pit?"

"Because we're friends, too," he hedged. "And I look out for my friends."

"Do you interrogate all your friends about their relationships?" she challenged.

"I'm not interrogating you," he denied.

"Are you sure? Because from where I'm sitting, it certainly feels like an interrogation."

"Then I apologize," he said, his tone stiff.

"Thanks for the ride," she said, when he pulled into her driveway.

"Anytime," he said.

But she'd already slammed the door in his face.

Susanna was usually pretty even-tempered, but there was no denying that Dean's questions about Roger had gotten under her skin. The cowboy had never shown any interest in dating her, but suddenly the idea that someone else might be interested had his lasso in a twist.

I don't think your cowboy is simply protective of you. I think he's jealous.

Remembering Marty's words, Susanna found herself wondering if it was possible that they might be true.

Not that she actually wanted Dean to be jealous—she just wanted to know that he cared enough about her that he could be.

Sometimes friendship can lead to more.

For eight years, she'd been hoping and praying that it was true, that the day would come when Dean looked at her and finally saw her as more than a friend.

Obviously today was *not* that day.

But today she had promised to do him a favor, so she calculated the time it would take him to get home before she sent him a text message, waiting to ensure that he wouldn't be distracted while he was driving.

You forgot to leave your Christmas gifts with me.

He immediately replied:

I wasn't sure you'd still be willing to help me wrap them.

I said I would.

Yeah, but that was before...

Before you were an ass?

Yeah.

Well, at least he was willing to admit it.

If you're going to be in town tomorrow, you can drop them off. I've got rehearsal in the afternoon, but my mom will be home.

Are you sure you don't mind?

She didn't mind. Besides, she would never renege on a promise. But she deliberately waited two minutes before responding. Just long enough—hopefully—for him to realize that he shouldn't take her for granted.

It's fine.

Because she'd never been able to refuse him anything.

Was she a fool?

Probably.

Did she let him take advantage?

Perhaps.

Was she making a mistake?

No.

Of that she was certain.

Because despite his recent obnoxious behavior, they *were* friends, and friends were willing to help out one another.

And maybe, just maybe, in the process of helping out a friend, he'd finally realize how lucky he was to have her in his life—and that he couldn't live without her.

Susanna tucked her phone into her back pocket and made her way into the kitchen. After she filled the kettle and set it on the stove to boil, she found her gingerbread recipe and began gathering the necessary ingredients.

"Late night tonight," her mom commented, shuffling into the kitchen in her favorite robe and fuzzy slippers.

She nodded. "Chuck wasn't happy with the transition between a couple of scenes, so he had us run through a bunch of different options." She pulled a second mug out of the cupboard for her mom. "Peppermint, lemon or chai?"

"I never drink chai this late at night," Joyce reminded her.

Which Susanna knew, of course, but her mind had been wandering.

"Peppermint or lemon?" she prompted.

"Lemon," Joyce decided. "Did Roger give you a ride home?"

"No, Dean did."

"What was *he* doing at the theater?"

"Picking me up." She poured boiling water into the mugs.

"Hmm."

"Don't," Susanna warned.

"Don't what?" her mom asked, the picture of innocence spoiled by the twinkle in her eye.

"Don't start speculating that his actions mean anything more than that he was feeling guilty because I didn't have time to get my car before rehearsal," she said, as she began measuring flour.

"You can't blame me for hoping that you'll meet a nice man—and it's not going to happen if you spend all your time in the theater."

There was no point in Susanna telling her mom that meeting a man wasn't her greatest ambition in life, because she did want to meet someone special, fall in love, get married and have a family. She just didn't think it was a quest to which she should devote all of her time and attention.

"Maybe I'll meet a man in the theater," she said instead.

"I guess that's a possibility," Joyce acknowledged, though she sounded dubious.

"Since we're on the subject of the theater," Susanna told her, eager to shift the conversation away from her lackluster love life, "there's a party for friends and family at the theater after our last show on the twenty-third, if you'd like to come."

"Oh." Joyce seemed surprised by the invitation. "Of course I'd like to, but…um… I've got plans for the twenty-third."

"What kind of plans?" Susanna pressed, her curiosity piqued by the uncharacteristically vague response.

"Didn't I mention the secret Santa party at Lorraine's house?"

"You did," she confirmed. "And you told me it was on Christmas Eve."

"Well, I was mistaken about the date—it's actually on the twenty-third."

"Then we can go to the Abernathys on Christmas Eve?"

"Actually… I've got plans for the twenty-fourth, too."

"With Ted," Susanna realized, naming the widowed rancher that her mom had been dating, albeit sporadically, for the past ten months.

"Do you mind?" Joyce asked, sounding worried.

"Of course I don't mind," she said. "As long as he makes you happy, I'm happy."

"He's taking me to meet his daughter and son-in-law and their kids," her mom confided, watching as Susanna mixed the wet and dry ingredients together. "You're invited, too."

"Meeting the family," she mused. "That's a big step—and no, thank you."

"I wish I'd said 'no, thank you,' too," Joyce confided.

"Why?"

Her mom lifted a slender shoulder. "Because things are good right now with me and Ted, and I can't help feeling that things will change—his expectations will change—if we start spending holidays and special occasions together."

"Isn't that one of the perks of having a boyfriend—a guaranteed date for family weddings and other important celebrations?"

"Maybe it's been you and me for too long," Joyce said, not directly answering her daughter's question. "Maybe I don't know how to let someone in to share my life."

"Lucky for you, Ted seems to know how and be willing to teach you."

"I am lucky," her mom agreed. Then she sighed. "But I felt lucky when I was with Ron, too. Like I was the luckiest girl in the world, because he loved me."

Susanna had heard the story of her parents' relationship before. She knew that they'd fallen in love almost at first sight and then raced to get married, eager to spend every day of the rest of their lives together.

They were married for a little less than a year when Joyce got pregnant—and only a few years after that, Ron was gone, having decided that the bright lights of Hollywood were more appealing than his wife and daughter.

Thinking about it now, Susanna began to better understand her mom's reticence in her relationship with Ted.

"When Ron left…when something like that happens—or at least when it happened to me—it's hard to trust the same words, the same feelings. Even if I believe Ted when he says he loves me, how do I know that I can trust that he'll stick around?"

"I think, if you love him, you just have to take a leap of faith."

"I do love him," Joyce confided. "But I'm not sure it's that easy."

Susanna wasn't sure that she was in a position to be giving advice about relationships to anyone, but thinking about what Dean had said earlier that day, she asked, "When you were with Ron—" she didn't like referring to her mom's ex-husband as her dad, because he hadn't filled that role for more than a few years "—when you pictured yourself ten or twenty years in the future, did you see him by your side?"

"No," Joyce admitted. "Although that might have

been the problem—that I was so busy living in the moment, I didn't look to the future."

"Think of your future now," Susanna urged. "Can you see Ted there with you?"

Her mom's lips curved slowly. "I can," she said. "I really can."

"Then maybe that's your answer," she said, as she wrapped the dough in cellophane to chill in the refrigerator overnight.

"I see something else, too," Joyce said.

"What's that?"

"You with a partner who loves every inch of you—and lots of grandchildren."

Chapter Eight

The door opened before Dean could knock, blasting him with the chorus of Jimmy Boyd's "I Saw Mommy Kissing Santa Claus."

"Somebody must have skipped out on his morning chores," Joyce Henry remarked, teasingly alluding to his early arrival.

"Nope. Just got an early start today," he told her.

"And I have yet to get started," she admitted, clearly heading out to work.

"Is Susanna up?"

She nodded. "Go on in," she urged. "She's in the kitchen."

"Thanks."

He took off his boots inside the door before following the sound of the music to find Susanna fully embracing the holiday spirit, swinging her hips to the music and singing along with Brenda Lee now.

She was in her usual uniform of jeans and what he suspected was a Christmas sweater, though the front of it was covered by a butcher-style apron with a gingerbread cookie and a speech bubble saying "Bite Me."

Nope.

He shook his head.

Definitely not going there.

"Hey," he said.

But Susanna just kept on singing. *"...later we'll have some pumpkin pie and we'll do some caroling..."*

Though he was very much enjoying the show, he suspected she wouldn't forgive him if he let it go on for too long, so he reached around to the back of the Google Nest Hub and tapped the volume button to turn the music down.

"...you will get a sentimental feeling when you— oh!"

He lifted a hand to wave, and watched her cheeks turn bright pink.

"Dean! Hi."

"Sorry if I'm interrupting, but your mom let me in on her way out," he said.

"It's not a problem," she said. "I just didn't expect you to show up this early."

"I thought if I came early, you might have time to help me with these," he said, gesturing with the bags he carried.

"I told you I'd help with your wrapping," she acknowledged, pointing with an icing bag toward the dining room table, half-covered with other boxes and bags. "But I didn't say *today*."

He dumped the packages where she'd indicated, then returned to the kitchen and took a seat at the island to watch her work.

"Do you want coffee?" she asked, not lifting her gaze from the cookies she was decorating. "Pods are in the drawer under the Keurig."

"I wouldn't mind a cup," he said. "How about you?"

She shook her head. "I've reheated mine twice already—apparently I can't drink and decorate at the same time."

"Especially not when you're also dancing and singing," he added, and had the pleasure of watching her cheeks color again.

"But you're going to pretend you didn't see and hear that, aren't you?" she asked hopefully.

He set a mug under the spout and started his coffee brewing. "What's in it for me?"

"Help wrapping your Christmas presents," she immediately replied.

"That was a preexisting arrangement," he reminded her, as he carried his mug back to the island.

"Okay, I'll sweeten the deal," she said, and set one of the gingerbread cookies on a plate for him.

"An irresistible offer," he said, breaking a leg off the cookie and popping it into his mouth. "When did you have time to make these?"

"I made the dough last night when I got home, then rolled it out and baked the cookies this morning."

He frowned. "It was after ten when I dropped you off."

She shrugged. "There was no way I was going to go to sleep right away, anyway. I'm always revved up after being onstage, whether it's a performance or just a rehearsal."

"I can understand that," he said. "But when I want to relax, I usually turn on the TV or pick up a book."

"So do I," she admitted. "But I wanted to take cookies to rehearsal today, to make up for being late yesterday."

"You weren't late," he protested.

"No, but I wasn't early."

"Does time work differently in the theater?" he asked curiously.

"It does when Chuck's running the show."

He chewed on another piece of cookie. "People take advantage of your generous nature."

A wry smile curved her lips. "Funny, that's almost exactly what Marty said when he learned that I was late because I was Christmas shopping with you."

"You weren't late," Dean said again. "And did you tell Marty to mind his own business?"

"No," she denied. "Because I appreciate that he's looking out for me, too."

Dean scowled as he popped the last bite of cookie in his mouth. Something about the flavor nagged at him, and when he realized what it was, he scowled for a different reason.

"Wait a minute… Isn't there molasses in gingerbread?"

She nodded. "Along with a whole bunch of other things."

"You said that you're allergic to molasses."

"That doesn't mean I can't bake with it," she hedged.

"But I've seen you eat gingerbread," he said. "After Christmas last year, when we finally got to break down that elaborate—and delicious—gingerbread house you brought into the office."

She shrugged. "Okay, obviously I lied about being allergic."

"Why?" he asked, baffled.

"Because you were about to force-feed me a piece of your cookie and I didn't want it."

"I wasn't going to force-feed you."

She gave him a disbelieving look.

"Probably not," he amended. "But I only wanted you to try it because it was a really good cookie and my mom taught me to always share."

"I'll be sure to tell her that you learned that lesson," Susanna said lightly.

"I'd rather you told me why you so adamantly refused the offer."

She shrugged. "I just wasn't in the mood for a cookie."

Her explanation wasn't very convincing, so he tried again. "You know there's nothing you can't talk to me about, right?"

"I know," she said.

Except it was obvious to Dean that she was still holding back about something, and he'd never known her to hold back before. But he decided not to badger her about it—not right now, anyway. He wasn't making any promises about the future, though.

Instead, he said, "Speaking of cookies... My mom said that she invited you to her Christmas Eve dessert extravaganza—and that you gave a noncommittal response."

"Between now and December twenty-third, my focus will be on the play. After that, I'll be able to make plans. But my Christmas Eve plans might be wrapping presents," she warned.

"How about this—I'll come here earlier on the twenty-fourth to help with the wrapping, and then I'll take you to the Flying A for a sugar high unlike anything you've ever experienced."

"I'll think about it."

Which, he knew, was exactly what she'd said to his mom.

And while he wasn't entirely surprised by her response, he was still disappointed.

"Since I'm here, I feel as if I should apologize again for expressing my obviously unwelcome concern about your relationship with Roger last night."

"Your concern is appreciated," she told him. "It's your method of expression that could use some work."

"I just don't want you to get hurt again."

"I promise, you don't have to worry about me falling for Roger. And I don't think he's interested in me that way, either."

"I wouldn't be so sure," he cautioned. "You've

got a lot going for you. You're smart and talented and beautiful."

She seemed surprised by his response. "Do you really think so?"

"All that and a whole lot more," he told her.

"And yet," she mumbled under her breath.

"And yet what?"

Susanna shook her head. "Nothing."

So he finished his coffee and got up to put the empty mug in the sink. "Well, since we're obviously not going to be wrapping presents today, I should probably head back to the ranch."

"Before you go—" Susanna found a snap-top container and filled it with gingerbread cookies for him.

Sunday's rehearsal went surprisingly smoothly, and Chuck rewarded the cast and crew by dismissing them before eight o'clock.

"A free evening," Susanna mused. "What am I going to do with myself?"

"Come out with us for pizza," Roger said.

Pizza.

One of Susanna's all-time favorite foods—all that chewy dough and tangy sauce and gooey cheese.

All those calories.

She opened her mouth to decline the invitation, because she knew it would be easier to say no to Roger now than to turn down a slice—or two—when they were at the restaurant, but Marty spoke up before she could.

"We'll be there," he said. "I just want to discuss a couple of things with Susanna first."

"Great," Roger said, his eyes still on Susanna. "I'll save you a seat."

She managed a smile for Roger, and when he'd gone, turned to glare at Marty. "I think one of the things we need to discuss is not speaking on behalf of someone else."

"This is the third time everyone has gone out after rehearsal, and you already skipped the first two times."

"I'm not a big fan of pizza," she said.

Marty gave her a look that clearly communicated disbelief.

"And maybe I've got other plans," she suggested as an alternative.

"Unless it's an actual date with your hunky cowboy, you're not getting out of this," he told her.

"He's not *my* cowboy," she said again. "And okay, I don't have plans, but it's late and I have work in the morning."

"Theater is about community," Marty reminded her. "These informal get-togethers are just as important as scheduled rehearsals for building camaraderie."

"I know. It's just that—" she sighed "—a slice of pizza contains at least four hundred calories."

"You probably burned off at least that many during rehearsal."

"Maybe," she acknowledged. "But—"

"And Irene Krecji is a nasty woman who's pissed at you because her daughter didn't get cast in your play," he interjected.

"I didn't realize Alicia had auditioned," she said, startled by this revelation. "Or that she was even back in Bronco."

Marty nodded. "Chuck called me in to read with her. Twice."

"Twice?"

"She totally blew it the first time, but Irene talked to the director and got her a do-over."

"And the second time?" she asked curiously.

"Not much better than the first. I think she was nervous. She admitted that it's been a few years since she last performed in high school."

"That would be more than a few years," Susanna said. "Because she graduated when I did."

"No wonder she was rusty," he mused. "And you can stop pretending you're not happy to hear that she was rusty."

"I wasn't even pretending," she said, letting the smile spread across her face. "Now—are we going for pizza or not?"

"There's one more thing I wanted to talk to you about first," he said.

"What's that?"

"Roger."

"I know he doesn't have a lot of acting experience, but I thought he did a really good job today."

"If I had concerns about his performance, I'd take them to Chuck," Marty said.

"So what are you concerned about?"

"The fact that the man has a Montana-sized crush on you."

"He does not," Susanna immediately denied.

"He does," her costar insisted. "And while I know you're not the least bit interested in him, I'm asking you to not break his heart before the play has run its course."

"I'm not ever going to break his heart," she promised.

"I don't care about ever. Just don't do it before December twenty-third."

"Susanna's theater group came into Bronco Brick Oven Pizza after rehearsal last night," Weston told Dean, as they were riding out to deliver hay and break up the ice on the pond so the cattle would have access to water.

"I thought you had a date last night."

"I did," his brother confirmed.

"Don't tell me you took her to a pizza place for dinner," he said, because he absolutely was not going to play into his brother's hand and ask about Susanna.

"It was Carly's choice."

"So...how was the date?"

"It went well," Weston said, making no effort to hold back the smile that spread across his face.

"You went home with her," Dean guessed, shaking his head.

"What can I say?" His brother shrugged. "I'm simply a man, unable to resist the invitation of a willing woman."

Dean had no response to that—or none that wouldn't be completely hypocritical, so he remained silent. Because regardless of his own past, he was ready for a relationship that meant something now.

Of course, he had to meet the right woman first.

Or maybe he already had.

Because lately, whenever he thought about his future, the woman he saw by his side looked remarkably like Susanna—and the idea of finally finding a woman who could fit into his life as perfectly as she already did was both exhilarating and terrifying.

"You know, if you left the ranch every once in a while, you might have reason to smile, too," Weston said to him.

"I leave the ranch," Dean responded. "I just don't see the point in meaningless hookups anymore."

"You mean since last New Year's Eve?" his brother challenged.

"Bianca was more than a hookup."

"Why? Because you hooked up with her several more times over the next few months?"

He chose to ignore the question, saying instead, "I think I'm finally at the point in my life that I'm ready to settle down. To share not just a few hours but my life with someone."

"Whoa," Weston said. "When did you become an old man?"

"Joke all you want—you're only two years younger than me."

"Yeah, but at least I'm still getting some action."

Susanna was in the staff room at Abernathy Meats, making a pot of coffee because someone—probably Garrett—had left the carafe with only dregs in the bottom, when Crosby walked in the next day. She knew darn well that every one of the men who were in and out of the offices knew how to make a pot of coffee, they just couldn't be bothered.

"It tastes better when you make it" was the excuse that Tyler always gave her.

Which was patently ridiculous because she'd bought cases of individual packets of coffee so that no one had to measure out the grounds. All any of them had to do was fill the reservoir with water, dump a packet of coffee in the filter and hit the button clearly marked 'Start.'

"I heard that you and Roger were pretty cozy at Bronco Brick Oven Pizza last night," Crosby remarked in a playful tone.

It was an effort to keep her focus on him when her eyes wanted to flit over to Dean, who was standing at the window with a mug of dark roast from her Keurig.

"Is that what he said?" she asked, uncomfortable

thinking that Marty—and Dean—might have been right about the actor having a crush on her.

"Nah, he'd never kiss and tell," Crosby said. "It was Weston who told me."

The brother in question walked into the room. "What did I tell you?"

"That Susanna and Roger were up close and personal at the pizza place last night."

Weston sent a guilty glance in her direction.

"I didn't say it like that," he protested, though not very strenuously.

"I didn't know you were there last night," she said.

"The place was pretty packed," Weston acknowledged.

"Which is why there were ten of us squeezed around a table for six," she felt compelled to explain, despite the fact that it was really none of his—or any of their—business.

"And only nine chairs?" he teased. "Is that why you were sitting on Roger's lap?"

She felt her cheeks grow hot. "I wasn't sitting on his lap."

Not for more than a few seconds, anyway, when she'd returned to the table after a visit to the ladies' room and discovered that Liz had moved into the seat she'd vacated.

Which didn't bother Susanna at all. She would simply take what had been Liz's seat at the other end of the table, between Marty and Avery. But as she went to move past Roger, he'd caught her around the waist and perched her on his knee.

It was all good-natured fun, and Susanna had responded by telling him that she only sat on the knees of men wearing red suits in the month of December, before extricating herself and moving to the vacant seat.

"Of course not," Weston said, with a conspiratorial wink.

"Leave her alone," Dean snapped at his brother. "She's not interested in Roger."

Susanna didn't know if she should be grateful for his defense or annoyed by his assumption.

"And now I'm going to sit behind my desk and get some work done," she said, and made a hasty exit.

She'd barely lowered herself into her chair when Dean followed her into her office. Her heart gave a traitorous bump against her ribs, as always, reminding her of the one-sided crush it had been nurturing for far too long.

"Sorry about my brothers," he said. "They can be idiots sometimes."

"You're all idiots," she told him.

"What did *I* do?" he asked, clearly taken aback by her response.

She sighed. "Nothing."

"I'm not such an idiot that I can't tell you mean *something* when you say *nothing*."

"Fine. If you really want to know, you have a habit

of jumping to conclusions and assuming you know things about me that you can't possibly know."

"Is this about Roger?"

No, it wasn't about Roger. It was about Dean and the fact that he'd somehow managed to figure out that his brother's friend was interested in Susanna but, after more than eight years, he had yet to figure out that she was in love with him.

Of course, there was no way she was going to admit any of that to him now. Instead, she said, "Why would you say I'm not interested in him? How could you possibly know?"

Dean lifted a shoulder. "He just doesn't seem your type."

"As if I've dated so many guys that I have a type," she said dryly.

He frowned. "Are you saying that you *are* interested in Roger? Is that why you were out with him last night?"

She huffed out a breath. "I wasn't *with* Roger. The whole cast was there."

"But you just said—"

"I didn't say anything," she interrupted, practically boiling over with frustration. "You're jumping to conclusions again."

"I'm sorry that I can't stop myself from wanting to look out for you," he said.

"I understand that you're only expressing brotherly concern," she assured him. "But you're not my brother and I'd appreciate it if you'd stop acting like you are."

He nodded. "You're right. I'm sorry."

But she didn't want an apology.

She wanted him.

Chapter Nine

"Don't you have anything better to do on a Saturday night than hang out with your big brother?" Garrett asked, opening the door of his cabin wider to allow entry to Dean—and the six-pack he carried.

"I could come up with any number of things," Dean assured him. "But it's too cold to want to go too far."

"I'm flattered," his brother said dryly.

Dean grinned as he shrugged out of his coat and dropped it, along with his Stetson, on the bench inside the door. "You got any food to go with the beer?"

"Didn't I sit across the table from you at dinner not even two hours ago?"

Although four of Hutch and Hannah's sons had built their own houses on the ranch property—Weston being the sole outlier—they all still gathered at the main house on Saturday nights—actually most nights, in truth—to have dinner as a family.

"That was two hours ago," Dean echoed.

Garrett shrugged, unable to dispute the point. "I've got chips and salsa. Maybe a frozen pizza."

"Chips and salsa will do," Dean said, following his brother to the kitchen.

Garrett found the bag of chips in the pantry and a jar of salsa in the fridge and handed both to his brother.

"Apparently you've been living on your own so long, you've become completely uncivilized."

As soon as the words were out of his mouth, Dean wished he could take them back. Because the only reason that Garrett had been living on his own was that his marriage had fallen apart.

Not even Dean was privy to the details about what had gone wrong—and truthfully, he wasn't sure he wanted to know—but there was no denying that Garrett had been a changed man after his wife left. The always quiet and responsible older brother had become downright serious and withdrawn, and Dean could hate Mackenzie for that alone.

Thankfully, Garrett seemed unfazed by his flippant remark. "You expect me to serve them up on a silver platter?"

"Not a silver platter, but a bowl would be good."

"You've been here often enough to know where they are," Garrett said, popping the tops off two bottles of beer.

Dean opened the bottom drawer to retrieve a couple of bowls. Then he tore open the bag of chips and emptied it into the big bowl and dumped half the jar of salsa in the other. He carried the snacks into the living room and Garrett followed with the beer.

He glanced at the TV, made a face. "You were watching the news?"

"Game hasn't started yet," his brother pointed out. "And it's good to know what's going on in the world beyond the Flying A."

Dean set the bowls on the reclaimed-wood coffee table and took a seat on the sofa, where he'd have easy access to the chips. "You could see for yourself if you left the ranch every once in a while," he said, in an echo of the sentiment Weston had expressed to him only a few days earlier.

"I meant the world beyond Bronco even," Garrett said, setting the bottles on coasters—proving he wasn't completely uncivilized, after all. "Although the big news seems to be local."

"What's that?"

Garrett lowered himself onto the sofa beside his brother and picked up the remote. "A major winter storm is heading this way."

"Maybe we should move the cattle from the north pasture so we don't have to trek so far to feed them," Dean suggested.

His brother nodded. "And the stream in the east pasture doesn't freeze over, so they'll have access to water."

"It sounds like we're going to be busy tomorrow." Dean scooped up salsa with a chip. "Whoever claimed Sunday should be a day of rest wasn't a rancher."

"But tonight, we've got hockey," Garrett noted, as the puck was dropped at center ice.

Dean tried to pay attention to the action on the screen. The Jets and the Wild had a decent rivalry, which usually translated into a good game, and yet, he found his attention wandering.

Susanna would be at the theater now, as she'd been every other night this week, and he wondered what Christmas sweater she was wearing today.

She had quite the collection—some of them with subtle patterns, others not subtle at all. Yesterday's sweater had an image of a gingerbread cookie wearing a Christmas sweater on which was an image of a gingerbread cookie wearing a Christmas sweater and so on.

Thursday's sweater had been a blue knit with a big white-and-silver snowflake. The day before that, she'd sported one with a Christmas tree with lights that actually lit up and a twinkling star on top. Marty had come into the office that day to run lines with her during her lunch break, and Dean had overheard the man asking her to turn it off, because how could he be expected to focus on running lines when his attention was riveted on her breasts?

Okay, he'd actually said that his attention was riveted on the lights, but Dean knew what he really meant.

Because behind the lights were Susanna's breasts, giving glorious shape to the Christmas tree.

How had he never before noticed that she had such mouthwatering curves?

And what the hell was he doing noticing them now?

This was *Susanna*.

She was practically part of the family and, okay, while actually not related to him in any way, she was way too young for Dean to be lusting over.

And for Marty Trujillo to be lusting over.

Roger was much closer to her age, but Susanna had admitted that she wasn't interested in Roger.

Hadn't she?

"Have you ever wondered how it's possible to know someone for a number of years and then suddenly find yourself wondering if you really know her at all?"

Despite the question coming out of the blue—and during a spectacular tilt on the ice—Garrett didn't seem to have any difficulty following his brother's train of thought.

"You're talking about Susanna," he guessed.

Dean didn't deny it. "I blame Marty. She's been different since he's been around."

"I don't know that it's Susanna who's different," Garrett remarked mildly. "But I do know that Marty isn't your problem."

"Because I don't have a problem."

"Yeah, you keep telling yourself that," his brother said, sounding amused.

"Why do you think I have a problem?" he demanded.

"I don't think, I know."

Dean tipped his bottle to his lips.

"Maybe you don't want to hear what I have to

say," Garrett continued. "But since you brought up the subject, I'm going to tell you, anyway."

"Please do," Dean said, the words dripping with sarcasm.

"Susanna's been in the wings for a long time, waiting for you to notice her, while you remained oblivious," Garrett said. "Now there are other guys who see her there, and you're having to consider the possibility that she might not always be around—and realizing that when she moves on with her life with someone else, there's going to be a great big hole in yours where she used to be."

It was an uncomfortable truth that Dean didn't want to acknowledge. Instead, he rose to his feet. "I'm going to get another beer. You want one?"

"Sure," Garrett agreed, with a nod. "But don't think that getting drunk will stop you from thinking about her."

Something else that Dean didn't need his brother to tell him.

Winona silently tiptoed into the kitchen—a skill she'd learned only after moving out of her own home in Rust Creek Falls and in with her daughter and granddaughter in Bronco. Prior to that, she'd stomped around at will at all hours of the night, because there'd been no one else around to hear her.

She much preferred tiptoeing.

She quietly filled the kettle with water and set it

on the stove to boil, then retrieved a mug from the cupboard and dropped a teabag into it.

Should she ready a second mug?

Sometimes Dorothea or Wanda heard her moving around in the kitchen, despite Winona's best efforts to be quiet.

But no. She wasn't going to have company tonight.

Her daughter was sleeping soundly, and her granddaughter wasn't yet home from her date, though she'd no doubt sneak into her own house in the early hours of the morning, as if she was a teenager out past curfew.

Only a year ago, Winona had been alone, not unhappy with her life but not feeling much joy, either. Her health had been failing, and she'd been all but certain the end was near.

But everything had changed when Melanie Driscoll—now Abernathy—had shown up at her door with visitors. In that moment, Winona had known that her life was about to change, though she hadn't known how completely.

She smiled as she poured boiling water into her cup, marveling at the fact that she was one of three generations of women living under the same roof.

Of course, she expected that the number would be down to two before the end of summer. Maybe even sooner than that. Because Sean was going to ask Wanda to marry him—not for the first time—and this time, Wanda was finally going to say yes.

Which meant another wedding to look forward to, another outfit to buy. Perhaps she'd go back to that fancy boutique and let Sofia help her pick something out—and maybe add a turquoise feather boa this time.

The cast of *A Christmas Wish* did a pretty clean run-through of Act One the next afternoon while the crew tinkered around in the background, putting the finishing touches on the set. Then the actors were given a five-minute break so that Chuck could discuss the music with the sound guy, and Susanna and Avery had just taken their marks onstage again when the theater manager came in, holding a box high in the air.

"The playbills are here," Mabel announced in a sing-song voice. "And they look fabulous."

"It looks like the snow's here, too," Liz remarked, eyeing the fluffy white flakes that covered the theater manager's hat and the shoulders of her coat.

"It is indeed," Mabel said. "At least six inches have fallen already, with a lot more predicted. Maybe it would be a good idea to cut rehearsal short today."

That drew Chuck's attention—and a scowl.

"I'll check it out," he said, instructing the actors to "carry on" while he went to peek outside.

So Susanna and Avery ran through their scene.

"What's your Christmas wish this year?" Avery—as Joy—asked Susanna's Holly.

"The same as last year," Holly confided to her

best friend. The wistfulness in her tone came easily to Susanna, because it was how she felt when she thought about Dean—the focus of her own Christmas wishes.

"That Noel will finally see you as something more than a pal?" Joy guessed.

"Is it such a fanciful wish?" Holly wondered.

"I don't know," her friend said. "But I think maybe it's time to stop wishing and take action."

"What do you mean?" Holly asked.

Of course, Susanna knew what the answer would be—unfortunately, she wasn't brave enough to actually follow the advice doled out by her own characters.

"I mean that you should tell Noel how you feel."

Before Holly could reply, Chuck returned to the stage.

"Unfortunately, Holly and Noel's happy ending is going to have to wait," he said. "Mabel's right. This storm looks as if it's going to live up to its billing, so I want everyone to pack up and head out now."

The actors and crew didn't need to be told twice.

"Susanna—can I ask a favor?" Chuck asked, as she was gathering up her belongings.

"Of course," she immediately agreed, noting that the usually calm director looked frazzled.

"My wife just texted and asked if I could pick up Liam. His basketball practice was cut short, and she doesn't want to have to drag the baby out in the storm."

"Go," she said, holding out her hands for the theater keys. "I'll lock up here when everyone is out."

"Thanks," he said.

She did a quick check of the theater first, walking up and down the front rows of seats, looking for forgotten items and tossing them in a bin beside the stairs where the owners could retrieve them the following day. Then she turned off all the lights, secured the doors and headed out.

By the time she exited the building, her vehicle was the only one remaining in the parking lot. And though she wasn't parked too far from the doors, the wind was strong enough that it took her breath away as she cut through the deepening snow.

She climbed behind the wheel, turned the key in the ignition and cranked up the heater and windshield defroster. Of course, she had to climb out again with her snowbrush to clear her windows so that she'd be able to see where she was going—at least as much as possible in the midst of all the blowing snow.

She carefully pulled out of the parking lot. Though she couldn't see the sides of the two-lane road, she figured she'd be safe so long as she followed the tracks left in the snow by other drivers who'd already come this way. Unfortunately, she'd barely made it half a mile down the road when her engine started to make a funny noise.

"Oh no." Susanna felt a chill all the way down to her bones that was unrelated to the storm raging outside. "Please, no. Please don't do this to me now."

But the car ignored her pleas, and simply and suddenly died.

She'd started to ease over to the shoulder when the noise started, so at least she was off the roadway. Not that there was any traffic, because apparently everyone else in Bronco had heeded the warnings about the storm and stayed home.

Susanna shifted her vehicle into Park, turned the key to the off position and dropped her head forward to rest it on the steering wheel.

"I'm not going to panic," she promised herself. "I'm going to give the engine a minute, then I'm going to restart it and continue on my way home."

It was a good theory, except that no matter how many times she pumped the gas and turned the key, the engine wouldn't turn over.

"Plan B." She dug her cell phone out of her purse to call for help.

No service.

Another side effect of the heavy snow, she was certain.

But staring at the message on the screen, Susanna felt herself begin to panic.

She drew in a deep breath and let it out slowly.

Okay…so what were her options now?

She could stay in her vehicle on the side of the road and risk freezing, or she could hike back to the theater where, even if the power went out—as frequently happened during winter storms—it was bound to be warmer than the inside of her car. Plus, there were old curtains and other textiles in the prop closet that she could use as blankets to stay warm. Not to mention a kitchenette with a refrigerator—and the possibility of food—and bathroom facilities.

The theater seemed like the preferable option—especially to her empty belly, except that she'd have to leave the safety of her vehicle and trudge through the blizzard to return to it.

And what if she got disoriented and wandered off-course?

No.

She refused to think negative thoughts.

More than once, her mom had remarked that Susanna spent so much time at the theater she could find her way there even if she was blindfolded, so she could certainly find her way in a snowstorm. And thinking of her mom gave her another reason to go back to the theater—to call Joyce on the landline and let her know that she was stranded but safe.

So she wrapped her scarf around her throat, pulled her hat down on her head, grabbed her backpack, pushed open the car door and stepped out into the cold.

And it was bitterly cold, with the added discomfort of icy flakes of snow coming at her from every direction and slashing at her face like tiny blades.

This wasn't a normal Montana blizzard—it was Mother Nature demonstrating her force and fury. It was the type of storm that caused people who were foolish enough to venture outside to lose their way and perish.

But Susanna wasn't going to lose her way. She knew exactly where the theater was, and even if she couldn't see the building through the blinding snow, she was 100 percent certain that she was headed in the right direction.

Or at least 90 percent.

But doubts started to creep in as she trudged onward, as what should have been a ten-minute walk stretched to almost twice that with the wind blowing in her face and the snow slowing her every step. Had she somehow gone past the theater? Had the storm thrown her off-course?

She put her head down and pressed on, refusing to let her worries and doubts turn her around. Instead, she continued forward, pausing frequently to catch her breath and squint into the distance.

I'm not going to panic.

With every laborious step, she repeated the words in her head, as if the process of saying them over and over again would make true.

And then, after what seemed like forever, she saw the outline of a building just ahead.

I made it.

Well, not quite yet, but she knew without a doubt now that she was going to be okay. And the sense of relief was almost overwhelming.

Just a little farther.

She urged her heavy limbs to keep moving.

Only a few more steps.

And then she was there, standing at the front doors that opened into the lobby. She hoped the key Chuck had given to her worked in this lock, because the backstage door was all the way around the other side of the building and she just wanted to get inside and out of the cold.

Her fingers, numb and stiff despite the fleece-lined mittens she wore, fumbled with the key, but she finally managed to insert it into the lock and wrench open the heavy portal.

Once inside, she automatically hit the switch beside the door, and exhaled a grateful sigh when the overhead lights came on.

There was power—and power was good.

There was also an ancient rotary phone in the kitchenette that Mabel refused to throw out, insisting that it was useful to have in case of emergencies.

Susanna rubbed her hands together, attempting to restore feeling in her fingers so that she'd be able to dial. But first, she needed a minute, and lowered herself to the floor before her trembling legs crumpled beneath her.

Chapter Ten

Hannah Abernathy was standing at the kitchen window, staring out at the snow-covered fields, when Dean walked into his childhood home Sunday afternoon.

"Are you worried about the storm?" he asked, when she turned around and offered him a weak smile.

She shook her head. "I'm worried about your brother."

"You'll have to be more specific—I've got four of them," he reminded her.

"As if I could forget," she said. "And though I worry about each of you at different times, this time it's Crosby."

"What did he do?"

"It's what he didn't do. He didn't come home last night."

He slid an arm across her shoulders. "He's thirty years old, Mom."

She sighed. "I know that, too."

"And how do you know that he didn't come home?" Dean asked, because she couldn't possibly see Crosby's house through the kitchen window.

"He texted to let me know that he was staying at Victoria's, so I wouldn't worry."

"And yet here you are," he pointed out.

"They've been dating for a while now."

He nodded. Three—or maybe four—months, which was a significant milestone for his usually commitment-averse brother.

"Do you have a problem with Victoria?" he asked cautiously.

"No," she said, though not very convincingly. "But I always hoped the day would come when he'd realize that Susanna is the perfect woman for him."

"Susanna?" Dean echoed dubiously.

"What's wrong with Susanna?" she demanded.

"Absolutely nothing," he assured her. "I just can't imagine—" didn't *want* to imagine "—her with Crosby."

"It's time for him to grow up and settle down."

Once upon a time, she'd been saying the same thing to Dean. Then he bought Whitney a ring—which she later gave back—and Hannah admitted that she felt responsible for his ill-fated engagement, that she'd perhaps pushed him to make a commitment he wasn't ready to make.

Truthfully, it was Whitney who'd pushed for the commitment, but maybe Dean had given in too easily because he'd believed it was time. In any event, his mom had mostly stayed out of his personal life since then, choosing to focus her attention on his brothers, instead.

"And I think Susanna would be good for Crosby," she continued now.

But would Crosby be good for Susanna? Dean wondered.

And why did it bother him that his mom wanted to set them up?

Because Crosby was right—he wanted Susanna for himself.

And wasn't this a fine time to finally accept that truth?

Of course, the more important question was: what was he going to do about it?

Joyce answered on the second ring, and the sound of her mom's voice—warm and familiar—brought unexpected tears to Susanna's eyes.

"Hi, Mom."

"Susanna, where are you? I thought you'd be home by now—it's really getting nasty out there."

"I'm at the theater."

"Still? You texted more than half an hour ago to say that you were heading home."

"My car died a little way down the road, so I came back. It looks like I'm going have to ride out the storm here."

"By yourself?" Joyce asked, sounding worried.

"Yes, Mom."

"I don't like the idea of you there on your own."

It wouldn't have been Susanna's first choice, either, but under the circumstances, she wasn't going to complain.

"I don't have cell service," she said now. "But so far, the theater landline is still working, so you can call me at this number if you want."

"I want to drive over there and bring you home," Joyce said.

"No!" Susanna immediately protested. "There's almost zero visibility outside, so I need you to promise me that you'll stay put until this storm passes."

Joyce sighed. "Okay, I'll stay put."

"Promise?"

"I promise." A buzzer sounded in the background. "Oh, that's the oven timer—our dinner's ready."

As if on cue, Susanna's stomach growled.

"I'll let you go have your dinner."

"But...what are you going to eat?"

"I thought maybe I'd call out for a pizza."

"I don't think they'll deliver in this weather," Joyce said seriously.

"I was kidding, Mom. Don't worry about me—I'll raid the refrigerator here."

"I will worry," her mom warned. "But only because I love you."

"I love you, too, Mom."

She replaced the receiver and drew a steadying breath, fighting against the tears that threatened again. Because crying wouldn't accomplish anything, and really, her situation wasn't so dire. She was safe from the storm, sheltered in a familiar place that had lights, running water and flush toilets.

Since she didn't know how precarious the power

situation might be, she decided to take advantage of it while it lasted. She filled the kettle with water and plugged it in. There were two kinds of tea bags in the cupboard—regular orange pekoe or decaffeinated Earl Grey. She opted for the Earl Grey.

When the kettle had boiled, she poured the water into the mug, then sat in one of the two mismatched chairs at the little round table that had an old playbill folded beneath one of its three legs to keep it balanced on the uneven floor. She wrapped her hands around the ceramic mug, and sighed as the warmth seeped into her skin.

As she sipped the steaming liquid, she considered calling a tow service about her car. But she imagined there were plenty of stuck drivers needing help, and while her vehicle was stranded out in the cold, she—thankfully—was not, so she decided to wait until after the storm had passed.

She'd just finished her tea and pushed away from the table to put the now empty mug in the sink when the overhead lights flickered.

She held her breath for several seconds, then exhaled on a sigh of relief when the power stayed on.

She'd always loved the theater. Not only because she'd made a lot of friends and happy memories here over the years, but also because the building itself was so full of character. The former Roman Catholic church had a wide balcony, soaring ceilings and lots of dark wood. It also creaked with every gust of wind and had numerous corners and alcoves where shadows seemed to lurk, and she imagined that it might be a scary place for a child alone.

Thankfully, she wasn't a child. She was a grown woman who wasn't afraid of the wind and wasn't going to jump at shadows.

But she did jump when she heard pounding on the door.

Then she froze in place, not sure what to do.

The one thing she did *not* want to do was open the door.

Suddenly being alone in the theater didn't seem so bad. Certainly it was preferable to sharing the space with a potential rapist or murderer.

Except she knew it was far more likely that whoever was pounding on the door was another stranded traveler seeking shelter from the storm. Someone who'd no doubt seen lights on, and she couldn't, in good conscience, leave them outside in the elements.

Still, she called out through the locked door first, "The theater's closed."

"Open up, Susanna."

Dean?

Her heart leaped with a dizzying combination of relief and joy.

She had no idea what he was doing here, but she didn't really care. She turned the dead bolt and wrenched open the door.

He was covered in snow, from the brim of the Stetson perched on his head to the boots on his feet, and he looked more like the abominable snowman than the handsome cowboy she knew. Still, she'd never been so happy to see him.

He stepped over the threshold and hugged her tight.

She hugged him back, not caring that she'd end up covered in snow, too.

"Are you okay?" he asked, drawing back to look at her.

"I'm fine." And now that he was here, she really was. "But—how did you know I was here?"

"Your mom called and told me that you were stuck here."

"She shouldn't have done that," Susanna protested. "I'm not a damsel in distress."

"Are you saying that you're not stranded?"

"I'm saying that I don't need to be rescued by a white knight just because my car broke down."

"A good thing," he told her. "Because I'm no white knight on a trusty charger, just a simple rancher in a truck with snow tires. But I'm willing to give you a ride home."

She didn't *need* to be rescued, but she wasn't foolish enough to turn down the offer of a ride from a friend.

"And I'm grateful," she said. "I just hate that you came out in the storm."

"Probably not as much as I hated the idea of you being stuck here by yourself," he said.

She sighed. "You just can't help but look out for me, can you?"

"Is that a problem?"

"No," she said, though not very convincingly. "But if you'd called instead of trekking over here in the middle of a major winter storm, I would have told you that I was fine."

"I tried calling," he said. "And my calls kept going directly to your voice mail."

"I meant you could have called the landline," she said. "That's how I contacted my mom."

"She didn't mention a landline," Dean said. "And, truthfully, I'm not sure it would have mattered. Because I was at the main house when Joyce called, and almost before I told your mom that I'd come get you, mine was handing me my keys."

"Apparently neither of them believes I can take care of myself," Susanna remarked.

"Or maybe they both love you and worry about you," he suggested as an alternative.

"You're right," Susanna said. "And I don't mean to sound ungrateful—"

"Then say 'Thank you, Dean,' and grab your coat so we can go."

Susanna grabbed her coat, because she was sincerely thrilled to know that she wasn't going to be stuck alone in the storm—especially a storm that didn't seem as if it was going to end anytime soon.

Though Dean had arrived at the theater not even three minutes earlier, apparently that was sufficient time for Mother Nature to kick it up another notch.

"The snow's coming down even harder and faster than when I got here," he noted grimly.

"Good thing you've got those snow tires, huh?" Susanna said, her tone hopeful.

"Snow tires only help keep the truck on the road—they don't miraculously increase visibility," he told her.

She sighed. "We're not going anywhere, are we?"

Dean shook his head. "I'm sorry."

And he was.

But he realized he wasn't nearly as sorry as he would have been if he'd let his mom send Crosby to the theater.

"Wait," she'd said, after Dean had told her his plan and headed to the door. "I just remembered that your brother's already in town. Maybe he can go get Susanna."

"Yes, he's in town," Dean had acknowledged. "With. His. Girlfriend."

"You don't think he'd want to help?" she'd challenged.

Of course he knew that Crosby would be happy to help. Because he cared about Susanna, as they all did.

"I don't think there's any reason to bother Crosby when I already said that I'd go," he'd told her.

"Well, if you're sure," she'd said, suggesting a hesitation that was at odds with the gleam in her eye.

A gleam that might have given him pause if he hadn't been so worried about Susanna.

But now that he was here, now that he knew that she was okay, he found himself wondering if this hadn't really been his mother's plan all along—or if all her matchmaking efforts in the past had made him paranoid.

"I'll bet you're wishing now that you hadn't answered your phone when my mom called," Susanna remarked lightly.

"Why would you say that?" he asked.

"Because I was always going to be stuck here overnight, but you thought you could play the hero and now you're stuck here, too."

"I'd rather be stuck here with you than be at the ranch, worried about you here all alone," he said.

"Because you don't think I can take care of myself, either?"

"I know you can take care of yourself," he told her. "But that doesn't mean I don't worry about you."

She didn't appear to be mollified by his response. "And now your parents are going to be worried about you, too."

"I should give them a call," he agreed, pulling his cell phone out of his pocket.

"No service?" she guessed, as he frowned at the screen.

"The storm must have taken out a cell tower." He tucked his phone away again. "You said something about a landline?"

"In the kitchenette," she said, leading the way.

The lobby wasn't very big, with a couple of small

rooms that served as a coat check and refreshment area when the theater was in use.

Susanna opened one of the double doors and stepped through into the auditorium, making her way down the center aisle to the stage. Previously an altar where the priest would have presided over mass, the platform had been raised up for better visibility and half a dozen steps added on either side for access.

"I've never been on the stage before," he confided, following Susanna up those steps.

"There isn't a show in progress, so you don't have to whisper," she said, sounding amused.

"Habit, I guess," he said, speaking in a normal tone.

Susanna guided him through the wings to the backstage kitchenette. She turned on the light and gestured to the ancient avocado-green phone secured to the wall.

"That's a blast from the past," Dean mused, lifting the receiver. "I'm pretty sure my grandparents had one just like this in their kitchen—and a fridge and stove in the same color."

"And no doubt they were the envy of all their friends."

"No doubt," Dean agreed with a grin, placing a fingertip on the rotary dial.

Susanna stepped out of the kitchenette to give him privacy for his call, which lasted only long enough for him to let his mom know that he was at the theater with Susanna and that they'd be there through the night, but he'd be home as soon as possible after the storm passed. Hannah promised to pass the same information along to Joyce and assured him that everyone at the ranch had hunkered down to ride out the storm and he shouldn't worry about anything but staying safe and warm and taking care of Susanna.

He'd just returned the receiver to its cradle when Susanna stepped into the room, her arms full of blankets. "Look what I found."

"Are we going to make a fort?" he teased.

She rolled her eyes. "I thought we should be prepared in case we lose power. It's comfortable in here now, but this old building can get drafty, and if the furnace goes out..."

He shuddered at the thought.

"Good thinking," he acknowledged. "We should probably see if we can find some candles and matches, too. Just in case."

"I've got something even better," she said, setting the blankets on the counter to show him the lantern she carried.

"Don't we need a candle to put inside the lantern?"

She shook her head. "It's battery-operated. *And* it has batteries inside that work."

"That is better," he agreed.

"And even if we don't have cell phone service, we've got flashlight apps on our phones."

"Hopefully we won't need them," he said.

She showed him her hand, fingers crossed.

"Now that the essentials are covered, why don't you give me a behind-the-scenes tour and tell me about your play?"

"You want a tour?" she said dubiously.

"Why not? We've got time on our hands and not much else to do."

"Okay, I'll give you the tour," she said. "But if you want to know what happens in the play, you'll have to buy a ticket just like everyone else."

"I've already got my ticket for opening night," he told her. "I just thought it would give us something to talk about."

"Since when do we have trouble making conversation?" she asked, leading him through the backstage area.

"Never," he admitted. "But maybe I'm curious about the story you wrote—and your inspiration. I was the kid who always hated writing essays in school, so I'm amazed by anyone who can put together a story."

"No one got excited about those 'What I did on my summer vacation' assignments," she assured him. "Except maybe the kids who went to Disneyland."

"But the topics Mr. Zold assigned in high school English were even more painful, requiring an 'exploration of theme' or a 'discussion of setting as character,'" he intoned in the teacher's pompous voice, then shook his head. "I still don't even know what that means."

Susanna smiled. "Confession time—I loved Mr. Zold's English class."

"Why am I not surprised?"

"It was Mr. Zold who told me that I had a talent for writing, who encouraged me to journal and even just jot down random ideas, insisting that everything has the potential to be a story."

"Is your play based on one of those random ideas?"

"No. Maybe." She shrugged. "It's a somewhat typical friends-to-lovers story."

"Friends-to-lovers, huh?" He seemed intrigued by the concept. "Is that something that happens a lot?"

"Probably more in fictional settings than real life," she acknowledged. "But when you're writing for the stage, you have to consider what's going to appeal to the widest possible audience in order to sell tickets."

They'd made their way around the backstage area while they chatted, with Susanna pointing out the dressing rooms and rooms for prop and costume storage.

"Of course, it's a holiday production, so the Christmas season is the obvious backdrop for the story," she told him now. "Because who doesn't love Christmas?"

"Scrooge?" he suggested.

"True," she acknowledged. "But that story has already been written."

"So there's no 'bah, humbugging' in your story?"

"No 'bah, humbugging,'" she confirmed. "But lots of traditional holiday elements—decorating Christmas cookies, wrapping Christmas presents, decorating a Christmas tree.

"Actually, I originally wrote the play as a novel,

so there were a lot of other scenes that had to be cut, like when Holly and Noel go ice skating and when they trek out into the woods to cut down the Christmas tree and when they rescue an abandoned dog."

"Why'd you have to cut those scenes?"

"Because we can't actually have an ice rink on the stage—or a dog in the theater."

"I'd have to disagree about the dog," he said. "Didn't you see Maggie basking in the adulation of the crowd at the tree lighting?"

"Animals who work in the theater or onscreen have to be highly disciplined. Maggie's escapades over the past few months proved that she doesn't even know how to 'stay.'"

"That's a fair point," he acknowledged. "So there's no ice rink and no dog, but are there any sword fights or magic spells?"

She laughed. "We're a community theater, not a blockbuster studio."

"I'll take that as a no."

"Sorry to disappoint you."

"I'm sure I won't be disappointed," he told her.

"I appreciate the vote of confidence," she said. "Usually I love being onstage, but I'm nervous about this year's performance, because I'll be speaking my own words. And if the audience doesn't enjoy the show, that's on me."

"Is this the first play you've written?"

"No, but it's the first that I've submitted to the board of the theater company for production consideration."

"Obviously they liked it."

"Or maybe they were just tired of watching interpretations of *A Christmas Carol* and *The Nutcracker*."

He cringed, recalling the most recent performance of the latter. "Especially when the Sugar Plum Fairy can't dance."

Susanna chuckled. "But she looked good in the tutu," she pointed out.

Dean just shrugged. "So tell me about the other plays you wrote."

"There aren't any sword fights or magic spells in them, either," she said. "But there is romance. Each of the stories is different, but in the end, the main characters realize they're meant to be together."

He tilted his head and looked at her. "I don't think I ever realized that beneath those ridiculous Christmas sweaters beats such a romantic heart."

"I'm going to pretend you didn't say that."

"Why? There's no shame in being a romantic."

"You know I was referring to your comment about my sweaters."

"I know," he admitted with a grin.

"And they're not ridiculous, they're fun."

"We're going to have to agree to disagree about that," he said. "Tell me instead why you like to write happy endings."

Chapter Eleven

It was a question that Susanna had asked herself on numerous occasions. Though she enjoyed reading all kinds of books and watching movies from various genres, when it came to her own writing, there was always—aside from the one play she'd only ever shared with Callie—a happy ending.

She shrugged, as if she didn't know how to respond to his query. "Maybe I watched too many Disney movies as a kid."

"That's not an answer, it's a deflection," he chided.

"Perhaps," she acknowledged. "But I didn't think you wanted to hear about my dysfunctional childhood."

"Actually, I do," he said. "Because I'm only now realizing that, as good as you are at getting other people to talk about themselves, you're equally reluctant to talk about yourself."

"Because my life isn't really that interesting."

"Let me be the judge of that."

"Okay," she agreed, albeit with reluctance. "I guess I'd say that I write happy endings because I want to believe they can exist."

"Why do you doubt it?" he asked.

"Because my parents' marriage fizzled like a can of soda left out overnight—and almost as quickly."

He winced at that. "I forget sometimes how lucky I am to have grown up with two parents who are not only still together but still love one another, even after forty-five years of marriage."

"Not only do you have two terrific parents, but you've also got four pretty great brothers."

"The brothers you can have," he said, making her laugh.

But her expression quickly turned serious again. "For as long as I can remember, it's just been me and my mom. And we've done okay," she hastened to add. "But sometimes, when I'm around your family, I can't help but wonder how different things might have been if my dad had stayed—or if I'd had a brother or sister."

"How old were you when he left?"

"Five." She guided him through the wings to the stage. "And this—" she spread her arms wide "—is our set."

She turned to Dean then, and found his gaze on her, his expression thoughtful.

"We're going to get back to this subject later," he told her.

Susanna threw her arms out again. "Our set." Her tone was firm.

This time, he took the cue and glanced around. "It looks like a living room."

"It's Holly's living room," she told him. "What we call a box set." She crossed the set to open a door, then walked through it to another door and opened that one, too. "And this is Noel's office."

"All of the action happens in those two rooms?"

"Most of it. We do the outdoor scenes in front of a painted front cloth. Not only does it keep the cost down, but it allows set changes to happen at the same time behind it."

"I see the Christmas tree that you mentioned decorating," he said. "Does that mean you have to un-decorate it after every performance in preparation for the next one?"

"Thankfully no," she said. "Because decorating—and undecorating—a tree is actually very time-consuming."

"Believe me, I know," he assured her. "My mom demands all hands on deck when her tree is ready to be decorated, and it still takes several hours."

"How much of that is because you and your brothers are jostling and fighting about what ornaments go where?"

"I don't know what you're talking about. And if my mom told you—"

"Your mom didn't have to tell me anything," she interjected. "I saw it for myself when I stopped by a few years back to get your dad's signature on a purchase order."

"I remember now," he admitted, a little sheepishly. "You must have thought it was complete chaos."

"It was chaos—and it was wonderful," she said. "Holidays with my mom are usually a lot quieter. Nice, but quiet."

"Sometimes I think quiet would be nice," he agreed. "But with four brothers, I've never had a chance to find out."

He moved back to the living room set. "So this is the tree?"

She nodded. "That's the tree at the beginning of the scene." She touched her boot to the button discreetly hidden beneath the tree skirt, and the tree slowly made a 180-degree turn to reveal a decorated side. "And at the end of the scene."

"Clever," he noted.

"Our lighting guy is a genius."

"So all the scenes that you cut from your story to turn it into a play, they're just gone?" he asked.

"Not completely." She settled into one of the wing chairs that was part of the set. "They're revealed through conversation between the characters, as if they happened offstage. Holly talks to her BFF, Joy, or her neighbor, Star. Noel talks to Jack, and—"

"And if anyone in the audience was somehow unaware that it's a Christmas play, despite the cookies, the presents and the tree, the character names are a not-so-subtle reminder."

"Well, the characters had different names in the original story, but I changed them when I submitted the play for consideration as a holiday production."

She absolutely was *not* going to tell him that Holly

used to be Anna and Noel was originally Daniel, because even Dean couldn't be so clueless to not see the similarities between the names Susanna and Anna and Dean and Daniel, and start looking for a deeper meaning in the story.

"So how do Noel and Holly meet?"

She was usually happy to talk about her plays, but this particular storyline struck a little too close to home, and she couldn't help but worry—or maybe hope?—that Dean might realize he'd been her inspiration.

"They've been friends for a lot of years," she said vaguely. "And though Holly's been in love with him for almost as long, Noel never looked at her as a romantic interest until Jack—a buddy from college—comes to town for the holidays. It's only when Noel is forced to consider the possibility that he could lose Holly to Jack that he realizes he loves her, that he's always loved her."

"If Noel's that clueless, maybe he doesn't deserve Holly," Dean suggested.

She smiled. "Maybe he doesn't. On the other hand, I'm pretty sure he's not the only clueless guy in Montana."

"But he gets the girl anyway?"

She nodded. "He sees Jack take Holly into a jewelry store and, certain that Jack is going to propose to her, rushes in to tell her that she shouldn't marry Jack—she should marry him, because he loves her. He's always loved her."

"And she falls for that?" he asked dubiously.

"She doesn't fall for anything," Susanna said. "But she accepts his proposal, because she loves him, too."

"Wait a minute—if she's been in love with him all along, why didn't she ever tell him how she felt?"

It was a good question, and one that kept Susanna awake a lot of nights. "Because she's afraid to even hope that he might feel the same way, and she doesn't want her heart to be trampled by his size-twelve cowboy boots."

"You didn't mention that he was a cowboy."

She winced inwardly at the slip, but recovered quickly.

"Actually, he's the editor of a local newspaper," she said. "But the story's set in Montana, so of course he wears cowboy boots like everyone else."

"You're obviously invested in your characters to know even their shoe sizes," he remarked.

"I enjoy writing and acting," she confided.

"My parents would kill me if they knew I was asking, because you're an invaluable asset to the office, but I can't imagine that you find your work there either exciting or inspirational."

"I'm excited to get a paycheck every two weeks," she told him. "I have no interest in being a starving artist."

As if on cue, her stomach grumbled so loudly that there was no way for Dean to pretend he hadn't heard it.

"I, uh, didn't make it home for dinner," she confided.

"And I'll bet you didn't have anything substantial for lunch, either," he said.

An admonition that lost some of its impact when *his* stomach growled.

She lifted a brow.

He shrugged. "I planned to drop you off at your house and be back at the Flying A for my mom's roast beef dinner," he said.

"There might be some leftovers in the fridge," she said.

"Let's go take a look."

"We've got some chicken fried rice," Dean said, opening a plastic container and examining its contents.

"That's Avery's," Susanna said. "Or maybe Liz's. They ordered Chinese for dinner the other night."

"Looks like a couple of chicken balls, too," he said. "And some beef and broccoli—but mostly broccoli."

"A veritable feast."

"Is there a microwave?" he asked, glancing around.

"Unfortunately, no," she told him.

"How about cutlery?"

Now Susanna nodded.

"Then grab two forks—it's dinnertime."

Dean was already seated with the food containers spread out on the table when she returned with the cutlery.

"Take your pick," he said to her.

Susanna eyed the chicken balls—one of her favorites on the menu at any Chinese restaurant—but reached for the container of mostly broccoli. Though the sauce was congealed, the broccoli was still crisp and surprisingly tasty.

Dean pushed the container of rice toward her.

She hesitated.

"I thought you were hungry."

"I am," she said. "But rice is…"

"What?" he prompted.

"Carbs."

"So?"

"So I'm trying to cut down on carbs," she admitted.

"Why?" he asked, then immediately answered his own question. "So that you can be skin and bones like so many other women?"

"I don't want to be skin and bones," Susanna said. "But I wouldn't mind being a little less…curvy."

"Why?" he asked again, sounding genuinely baffled this time. "Your curves are—" He stopped and shook his head. "I'm sorry. This is a completely inappropriate conversation."

"Maybe, but now I want to know," she told him. "My curves are *what*?"

"I shouldn't have said anything." He dipped a chicken ball in cold sweet-and-sour sauce. "Your curves are none of my business."

Her gaze narrowed. "That isn't what you were going to say thirty seconds ago."

"No, it's not," he agreed.

She poked another spear of broccoli with her fork, but curiosity won out over caution, prompting her to ask, "So what were you going to say?"

Though Susanna would have sworn that nothing could make the rancher blush, she was sure she saw just a hint of color creep into his cheeks as he sighed.

"I was going to say that your curves are…" he paused to clear his throat "…sexy."

She blinked, stunned, as an unexpected thrill snaked up her spine.

Sexy?

"That's what you were going to say? Really?"

He nodded. "I've never understood why so many women want to look like models, with flat chests and jutting hip bones, because I promise you, most men want a woman with curves, who feels soft and warm in his arms."

"Says the man whose fiancée ordered a wedding dress in a size four," she remarked dryly.

"*Former* fiancée," he reminded her.

A clarification that did *not* inspire her to dig into the rice. Because no matter what Dean said now, he'd obviously been attracted to Whitney. Susanna, on the other hand, seemed only to attract leering glances and wolf-whistles, and not even those from the cowboy seated across from her.

Instead, she began gathering up the empty containers. "Did you want—"

"Shh." Dean held up a hand and strained his ears, listening.

Susanna stared at him, her jaw slack. "Did you seriously just *shush* me?"

At the risk of having them nipped, he gently touched his fingers to her lips to silence any further response. "Do you hear that?"

She shook her head.

But then she paused.

"Wait…is that…is someone…scratching at the back door?"

"More likely some*thing*," he told her.

"A dog?" she guessed.

He was already on his feet.

"What if it's not a friendly dog?" she asked.

"Friendly or not, I'm not going to leave a creature outside in this storm," he said. "Especially when he's trying so desperately to get in."

Susanna followed him to the door.

Along with the scratching, he could hear whining now.

Plaintive, almost desperate.

He wrestled open the door, and a furry creature bolted between his legs.

Definitely a dog.

"Oh, the poor thing must be so cold," Susanna said. She immediately grabbed a blanket from the pile and dropped to her knees to wrap it around the shivering animal. "Is it...ohmygoodness—it's Maggie."

"Houdini would have been a better name for that dog," Dean remarked, as the grateful pooch swiped her tongue over Susanna's chin.

She looked at him, her eyes filled with worry for the animal. "I thought she was back at Happy Hearts."

"Apparently she's got wanderlust in her blood," he said.

Maggie let Susanna fuss over her for another minute or so, then she pulled away and started to explore. She made her way to the front of the stage, then sniffed all around the desk that was the centerpiece of Noel's office before crawling beneath it, turning in a circle a few times and finally lying down on the rug.

"She looks exhausted," Susanna said sympathetically.

"She looks like she's getting ready to have her puppies."

"What? No," she protested. "She can't have her babies here. Not now."

"I don't think we can stop her," he said.

"But I don't know what to do—how to help her."

"You don't need to do anything," he assured her. "It's a natural process."

"Spoken like a man who won't ever have to push a baby out of his body," she noted dryly.

"Spoken like a rancher who's witnessed the births

of countless calves, more than a few foals and even
a litter or two of kittens."

"But no puppies?"

"We usually had male dogs at the Flying A—and,
male or female, they were always fixed so that they
wouldn't be tempted to venture too far from home."

"Should we do something to help?" Susanna
asked, when Maggie started to whine and move
around again.

"Only if she seems to be in distress."

"Doesn't she sound distressed to you?"

Dean put his arm across her shoulders. "She's
fine."

"But she's alone."

"She doesn't know us," he pointed out. "Yes,
she seems grateful that we brought her in out of the
storm, but forcing our attention on her during what
is already a stressful time might do more harm than
good."

Though Susanna was still worried about Maggie,
she had to trust that Dean knew a lot more about animals giving birth than she did.

Half an hour later, when Maggie had already delivered three puppies and was in the process of push-
ing out a fourth, Susanna had to admit that he was
right.

"She really doesn't need any help, does she?"

"Most animals don't," he told her.

"Is it normal for the puppies to cry like that?"

"It's not only normal, it's a good sign, because

it tells you that the lungs are clear and the pup is breathing."

"I guess dogs probably aren't so different than cows," she said. "Except that they're a lot smaller. And cuter."

"I can't disagree with the size part," he said. "But newborn calves are pretty darn cute."

"Still, they're not puppies," she said. "And Maggie just gave birth to number five." She shook her head, marveling over the fact.

"She's not done yet."

"Are you sure?" Susanna asked, surprised by his confident assertion. "How do you know?"

"Look at her belly," Dean said. "And you can see she's still having contractions."

"But…she's already got five."

"And that's a decent-size litter," he acknowledged. "But hardly unusual."

Maggie settled down then and closed her eyes.

"She looks done to me," Susanna said.

"Nah, she's just taking a break."

It turned out he was right about that, too.

It was two hours later before the entire birthing process was done and the exhausted mom was settled in an oversize box they'd found in storage, nursing her eight puppies.

"Eight. Puppies."

Dean chuckled. "You keep saying that."

"Because I still can't believe it."

"Daphne said that Australian shepherds usually

have litters of six to seven," he reminded her, because he'd ducked back into the kitchenette while Maggie was in labor to give the owner of Happy Hearts a call to let her know that the runaway had found her way to the theater and was safe.

Daphne had been frantic to learn that the dog was missing—again! Apparently one of her teenage volunteers had inadvertently let her out, but Daphne promised that she would come to the theater to pick up Maggie and her pups as soon as the storm was over and the roads cleared.

"But Maggie had eight," Susanna said again. "Obviously, she's an overachiever."

"I'm just glad the lights stayed on," Dean said. They had, in fact, flickered a few times as the storm continued to rage outside, but so far, they still had power. "It would have been a lot harder to keep track of what was happening in the dark."

The lights flickered again, and Susanna sighed. "Now you've done it."

"Done what?"

"Tempted fate."

And sure enough, the next time the lights flickered, the theater was plunged into darkness.

Chapter Twelve

As Susanna used the flashlight app on her phone to light her way to the lantern she'd left on the set, Dean followed her across the stage.

"You can't honestly believe this is my fault," he said.

She pressed the power button on the lantern and was rewarded with a soft glow of light.

"The way the wind is blowing, it was almost inevitable that the power would go out," he continued.

"Almost inevitable isn't the same as inevitable."

She began spreading out blankets on the floor.

Dean gave up trying to reason with her, instead helping her fashion a makeshift sleeping area.

"Too bad you didn't write a play where the action happens in a bedroom, then we'd have somewhere comfortable to sleep tonight."

"I write family-friendly romance," she reminded him.

"I'm just saying, a bed would be a lot more cozy than the floor."

On the other hand, it was probably a good idea there wasn't a bed on the set, because he had no business even thinking about getting cozy with Susanna.

So they sat on the floor, their backs against the twin wing chairs that were part of the set, listening to the wind howling outside.

"Now might be a good time to get back to that conversation we didn't finish earlier," he said.

"Like a dog with a bone," she muttered, not quite under her breath.

"Yep," he agreed, unapologetic.

She sighed. "So where did we leave off?"

He was pretty sure she knew exactly where they'd left off, since she'd dropped the topic like a hot potato, but he answered the question anyway. "You were five when your dad left."

She nodded. "He took off just a few days before my kindergarten graduation. Or maybe it was weeks. I'm not sure I had any real understanding of the passage of time back then.

"What I do know is that he was apparently spotted by a casting director on vacation in the area who suggested that his talents might be of use in Hollywood— his talents being riding a horse and roping a calf," she clarified. "He quit his job at Sunnybrook Ranch that same day, then came home and told my mom that we were moving to California.

"But she refused to go. My grandfather—my father's father—wasn't in the best of health, and she'd been helping my grandmother take care of him."

"So your mom stayed in Bronco to take care of your dad's parents?"

Susanna nodded again. "While they were alive,

my dad occasionally came back to visit, but he never again suggested that we should move out to California with him. And after my grandparents had both passed, he announced that he didn't ever plan to return to Bronco, because he was happier in Hollywood and had never really been cut out to be a husband or father, anyway. They were divorced six months later."

He shook his head. "I'm sorry, Susanna."

She shrugged. "It wasn't a fun time in my life," she acknowledged. "But my mom did her best to ensure that I never felt as if I was missing out because I didn't have a dad. And, in retrospect, she deserves a lot of credit for not completely freaking out when I first started to show an interest in acting, because that couldn't have been easy for her."

"Your mom is pretty great," Dean said.

"She is," Susanna agreed. "Which almost makes up for the fact that my dad is a complete dick who, despite working steadily as a stunt double in Hollywood, rarely ever made his child support payments."

He was surprised that this was the first time he was hearing any of this, then realized he probably shouldn't be. Because the shine of having a dad who worked in Hollywood was undoubtedly dimmed by the knowledge that the man had chosen his career over his family. Even now, it had to be painful for Susanna to talk about her father's abandonment, and he felt humbled that she'd entrusted him with the details.

"Did you know that I was once in a play?" he

asked, in an obvious effort to shift the conversation away from her unhappy childhood.

"I did not," she said, and managed a small smile.

"In sixth grade our class performed *Pinocchio*. I was a fish."

"A fish?"

He nodded. "In the underwater scene where Pinocchio gets swallowed by the whale. I wore a blue-and-orange costume, with my face sticking out of the fish's mouth."

Now she laughed. "Ohmygod—I've seen a picture of you in that costume. In the living room at your parents' house."

"What can I say? Mom and Dad were so proud."

That earned another soft chuckle, even as she drew her knees up to her chest and wrapped her arms around her legs.

"You're cold," he realized.

"A little," she admitted.

Which wasn't really surprising, considering that the temperature in the old building had noticeably dropped since the power went out.

"Come here," he said, patting the space on the floor beside him.

She hesitated for about half a second before scooting over, obviously accepting that sharing body heat was the logical thing to do.

It wasn't as if this was the first time they'd sat close together. Every time they went to see a movie together, their shoulders and thighs inevitably rubbed together. In addition, they'd shared the occasional hug over the past eight years. But this was different somehow, and they both knew it.

And as she snuggled against him, her head against his shoulder, her curvy body aligned with his, there was suddenly more heat coursing through his veins than Dean had anticipated. And maybe it was the normal reaction for a man in close proximity to an attractive woman, but this was *Susanna*.

He wasn't supposed to be thinking of Susanna as an attractive woman—or a woman at all.

She was a friend.

Almost like a sister.

But she's not your sister, a voice in the back of his head reminded him. *So there's absolutely no reason you can't kiss her.*

Don't do it, the rational side of his brain pleaded. *Kissing Susanna will change everything.*

Change is good. Necessary, even.

Dean felt as if he was Pluto in that old cartoon where the dog rescues a kitten from the pond and then gets conflicting advice from Devil Pluto— complete with horns and pitchfork—who wants him to kick the kitten out of the house, and Angel Pluto—wearing a halo and a dress—who urges him to play nice.

And apparently like Pluto, Dean wasn't going to listen to the voice wearing the halo.

Because when Susanna tipped her head back to look at him, obviously waiting for a response to something she'd said, all he could think about was the fact that her lips were *right there*. That barely a few scant inches separated his mouth from hers.

He only needed to dip his head and he could taste those sweetly curved lips that had tempted him for so long, despite all of his best efforts to pretend it wasn't true.

Not that he had any intention of breaching that distance.

Of course not.

Because this was *Susanna*.

No way would he ever—

Apparently the signals from his brain didn't make it to his mouth, because it was already brushing over hers.

And Susanna's lips were every bit as soft as he'd imagined.

Soft and sweetly responsive.

Tempting him to linger, to deepen the kiss, to ease her back onto the blanket and—

He drew back, appalled by the direction of his thoughts, and braced himself for the sting of her palm against his cheek, certain it must be coming.

Or perhaps the blow of a fist striking his chin.

Susanna didn't really seem like the slapping type. If she was mad that he'd overstepped, she'd let him know it in a more definitive way.

But she didn't hit him.

At least, not yet.

He tried to gauge her expression, but even with the glow of the lantern, it was too dark for him to see her clearly.

She seemed to be considering what had just happened.

Contemplating an appropriate response.

Then she lifted her hand to the back of his head and pulled his mouth down to hers again.

Susanna would never have had the courage to kiss Dean if he hadn't made the first move. And though it had started with a light brush of his lips, that fleeting contact had been enough to send sparks dancing through her veins as if they were live wires, making her head spin and her body yearn as the kiss she'd been waiting eight long years for finally happened.

When his mouth had finally—*finally!*—made contact with hers, she knew that this moment—and this man—had been worth the wait.

But no way was she going to wait another eight years for him to kiss her again, so she took the initiative this time.

Their second kiss was even hotter than the first, and their mutual passion quickly escalated. But just when she thought things were going to get interesting, Dean tore his mouth from hers, his breathing ragged.

"I'm sorry."

She blinked. "What?"

"Susanna… I can't… We shouldn't…" He seemed to be having trouble putting a complete sentence together and finished with another, "I'm sorry."

"Why are you sorry?" she asked cautiously.

"For taking advantage of the fact that we're trapped here together."

"A kiss is hardly taking advantage. And I know how to say no when I mean no," she told him. "And I'm not saying no."

"But I am," he said.

"Oh." Susanna drew back, stunned—and stung—by the firmness of his reply.

"I'm sorry," he said again.

As if an apology was supposed to somehow make everything okay.

Not likely.

She was grateful that the lantern was far enough away that her face was in the shadows, so that he couldn't see how much his rejection had hurt her.

"It's late," he said, after another minute had passed and she'd remained silent. "We should probably get some sleep."

She tapped her Fitbit to illuminate the display. 9:14.

Of course, it felt a lot later because of everything that had happened, including her car breaking down and having to trek back to the theater in the storm, so she reached up and pulled a decorative cushion off the chair, to use it as a pillow.

Then she turned her back on Dean and stretched out on the floor.

"Are you going to turn the lantern off?" he asked her.

"No."

"You're not afraid of the dark, are you?"

"No," she said again. "But it's a tradition to leave a ghost light on in the middle of the stage, at all times, even when the theater is empty."

"Why?"

"To appease the ghosts living in the theater."

He took a moment to consider that. "You're saying the theater is haunted?"

"All theaters have ghosts," she said matter-of-factly. "But the light serves a practical purpose, too. Backstage areas are notoriously cluttered with props and scenery, and keeping a light on at all times reduces the risk of accident and injury."

"Don't you think it makes more sense to conserve the batteries for when we actually need the light rather than waste it while we're sleeping?"

"It's not about sense, it's about tradition."

So the light stayed on.

Unfortunately, it didn't provide any heat and the floor wasn't only hard, it was also cold.

"Come here," Dean said, after she'd tossed and turned several times, trying to get comfortable.

"I'm fine where I am," she told him.

But Dean was apparently just as stubborn as she, because when she ignored his invitation, he simply grabbed hold of the edge of the blanket and pulled it—and her—toward him.

She instinctively stiffened as he shifted to align his front to her back.

"Relax," he urged. "I promise I can control myself."

"I never had any doubt," she assured him, in a tone that was chillier than the room.

But eventually his warmth did envelop Susanna, her breathing evened out and she drifted into slumber, happy to be in his arms, even if only because of the storm.

Susanna fell asleep snuggled close to Dean for warmth—and woke up horrified to discover that she was sprawled on top of him like a blanket. She didn't know how long she'd slept and there were no windows in the theater to tell her if it was still night or if the sun had risen. There was only the soft glow of the lantern.

She started to shift away from Dean, wanting to put some distance between them before he woke up and realized she'd climbed him like she was an adventurous preschooler and he was a jungle gym. But as she began to slide away, his arms tightened around her, holding her in place. It was then that she realized he wasn't only awake, he was aroused!

Her body immediately responded, a shot of pure, unadulterated lust shooting through her veins like a drug. Of course, she'd always been addicted to Dean, happier in his presence, practically giddy when he gifted her with his attention. Not that she was foolish enough to let him know it, but neither could she deny the truth to herself.

She would have expected the memory of his rejection the previous night to have tempered her response to him, but apparently her traitorous body was more forgiving than her bruised heart. Still, she wasn't so foolish that she'd give him a chance to shove her aside a second time.

Was she?

"You're…um…" She shouldn't have said anything, but she was so surprised by the evidence of his arousal, she spoke without thinking.

"Yeah." His voice was low, and a little rusty from sleep. "Sorry about that."

"It's okay." She kept her tone light, casual.

Nothing to see here.

No hormones ricocheting through her system.

Nope. She was cool.

Totally unaffected.

"I know it doesn't have anything to do with me," she assured him. "That a man's testosterone levels are highest in the morning and that even men who sleep alone can wake up with…um…"

"A hard-on?" he supplied dryly.

She swallowed. "Yeah."

"That might be true," he acknowledged. "It's also true that my testosterone levels were stimulated by the happy discovery of your sexy body in very close contact this morning."

"Wait a minute," she said, a furrow etched between her brows. "If you think I'm sexy —"

"It's not just an opinion but a fact," he told her. "You are an incredibly sexy woman, Susanna Henry."

The furrow between her brows deepened. "Now I'm really confused."

"What are you confused about?"

"If you're attracted to me…"

"I think it's been clearly established that I am," he acknowledged ruefully.

"Then why did you put the brakes on last night?" she asked.

"Because I didn't want to take advantage of the fact that you were stuck here with me," he said.

"I was happy to be stuck here with you. I mean, I wasn't happy to be stuck here, but since I was stuck, I was glad you were here with me."

"And I didn't want to take advantage of the fact that you were feeling grateful for my company."

"You can't take advantage of a willing woman," she told him. "And I know you have trouble remembering sometimes, but I'm all grown up, Dean Abernathy."

"I've noticed," he assured her.

"And I know what I want."

"Do you?" His gaze was focused and intense, as if looking for reassurance that *she* was sure.

She nodded.

She wanted Dean—she'd always wanted Dean.

But she was afraid that if she used those exact words, he'd somehow know how much she cared about him and he'd balk. Because he'd never want to mislead or hurt her. But if she made it clear that they were two consenting adults acting on a mutual attraction, she might finally realize her long-time fantasy of being with Dean.

Of making love with the man she loved.

"I want you, Dean," she said, and shifted so that she was sitting up, her knees bracketing his hips, then yanked her sweater over her head.

Of course, it wasn't the dramatic reveal that she was hoping for, because it was December in Montana and she was wearing a long-sleeved T-shirt beneath the bulky sweater. But she quickly dispensed with that, too, then twisted her arm behind her back, reaching for the clasp of her pink satin bra.

Dean sucked in a breath and caught her hands, halting her progress. "Wait."

But she'd been waiting too long already. In fact, she felt as if she'd been waiting her whole life for this moment.

For Dean.

But she waited, because he'd asked.

And because that single word opened the door just enough to let her age-old doubts creep in.

Had he changed his mind?

Maybe now that she was half-naked, he was having second thoughts.

Maybe—

"I'm trying to remember all the reasons that this is a bad idea," he admitted. "But right now, all I can think about is how much I want you."

She exhaled slowly. "Then why are we waiting?"

"Because I just…want to look at you," he said, drawing her arms down to her sides. "You are so stunning…so sexy."

He sounded as if he truly meant what he was saying. And the way he was looking at her made her believe that she was sexy. And the door slammed shut, locking out any lingering doubts.

Then those strong, tough rancher hands slid up her torso, caressing her body. His palms were rough and calloused, but his touch was gentle, almost reverent.

His fingertips traced the scalloped lace along the band of her bra, and she shivered, not with cold now but with anticipation. He hadn't touched her breasts, but her nipples were already peaked, aching. He traced the band around her back and unhooked the clasp, then gently drew the straps down her arms, allowing her breasts to spill free of their confinement.

"So." He let her bra fall away. "Incredibly." And lifted his hands to cup her breasts. "Sexy."

He circled her areolas, slowly, lazily. As if they had all the time in the world and he was happy to spend it exploring her breasts. And Susanna wasn't in any big hurry. Not really. But she'd been waiting for this moment—for *him*—for so long, and as she tugged his shirt out of his jeans, she kind of wished Dean would stop teasing and start touching. That he'd—

"Oh." Her head fell back and her eyes closed as the pads of his thumbs brushed over the aching peaks of her nipples, sending arrows of sensation from their tips to her very center.

Dean lifted his upper body off the floor then, so that they were both sitting up, chest to chest. He pulled her closer, so that her breasts brushed against the soft flannel of his shirt, the gentle friction arousing her further. Then he captured her mouth in a long, slow, deep kiss that made everything inside her tremble. And somehow, while he was kissing her, he eased her onto her back, so that he was on top now, and totally in control.

His lips moved across her jaw, down her throat.

Dean knew Susanna was self-conscious about her body, but to him, she was perfect. He took his time undressing her, marveling over the softness of her skin, the fullness of her curves. And her breasts...

Her breasts were quite simply spectacular. Round and plump and centered with dark pink nipples already tight at their peaks.

He took one of those nipples in his mouth. She sighed when he laved it with his tongue, gasped when he suckled it gently. He shifted to the other breast, ensuring that he gave it the same attention. Her breath was coming in short, shallow gasps now, and he suspected that he could make her come just like this, just by kissing and caressing her breasts.

Hell, the sexy noises she was making were almost enough to make him lose control.

Instead, he resumed his leisurely survey, moving slowly down her torso, his mouth trailing kisses over her silky skin. His fingertips skimmed down her sides, over the curve of her hips. He nudged her legs apart, then turned his attention to the sweet spot at the apex of her thighs. He parted the soft folds, pleased to discover that she was already wet and ready for him.

He brushed his thumb over her nub, and she gasped again.

Yeah, that was the sweet spot.

He continued his intimate exploration, making her moan and writhe, taking her right to the edge, to the point where she was gasping for breath. Then, and only then, did he get rid of his own clothing and rise over her.

He was rock-hard and aching, desperate to bury himself deep inside her, and it was habit more than conscious thought that had him reaching for the jeans he'd recently discarded, fumbling to find his wallet and the little square packet tucked inside.

She watched with avid interest as he sheathed himself with the condom, then she reached for him. Her hands eagerly explored his body, sliding over his chest, his shoulders and down his back.

The muscles in his arms quivered with the effort of holding himself over her as he fought against the primitive instinct to drive into her, hard and deep. Though he prided himself on ensuring that he satisfied a woman in bed, he hadn't always been a self-less or careful lover. But this was Susanna, so he was determined to be both.

He lowered his head to kiss her again, their mouths merging as their bodies joined together.

She lifted her legs to hook them at his back and tilted her hips to pull him deeper, and he groaned with the pleasure of being inside her. Finally. Completely. But she didn't give him much time to savor the sensation before she started to move, and they settled into a rhythm that carried them both into the abyss of pleasure.

Chapter Thirteen

Susanna had dreamed of making love with Dean far more often than she was willing to admit. But even her most vivid and erotic dreams paled in comparison to the reality of being in his arms, and she almost wished the storm would continue to rage on, so that they could stay right where they were, together, naked in each other's arms.

But that was a selfish and—she realized when Maggie whined—an unrealistic wish, and she managed to stifle her sigh of regret when Dean began to gather up his clothes.

"Are you taking her outside?" Susanna asked worriedly.

"I'm going to open the door and let her go outside," he said. "Provided that the snow hasn't piled up against the door, trapping us in here."

"The back door should be okay," she said. "The way the wind usually swirls around the building, it usually stays clear."

"Let's hope you're right."

"But…what if she takes off again?"

"I don't think she's going to abandon her pups," Dean said.

But because Susanna was concerned, he found a length of rope and tied it to the dog's collar. While he was fashioning the knot, Maggie was watching him, her canine expression somehow managing to express exasperation, but she sat obediently and let him complete the task.

Nature was calling for Susanna, too, so while Dean was dealing with the dog, she wrapped herself in a blanket and made her way to the bathroom.

Maggie was already back inside and nursing her puppies again when Susanna made her way past the desk area the dog had claimed as her own. It was the cold more than the darkness that told her the power was still out.

"Do you think they're going to be okay?" she asked Dean worriedly. "The temperature has really dropped in here."

"They're huddled together for warmth and comfort," he said, even as he covered part of the box with a blanket, tucking it beneath the bottom of the container. "Which is what we should be doing."

She tapped her Fitbit.

4:37.

"I don't imagine anyone will be knocking on the door anytime soon to rescue us?"

"Not anytime soon," he confirmed. "And while it's still snowing, the wind has really died down, so hopefully the worst of the storm has passed."

They settled back onto their sleeping pallet, and Susanna snuggled closer to the warmth of Dean's body.

"I can already tell that I'm going to be sore tomorrow—or later today," she mused.

"This floor is pretty unforgiving," he acknowledged. "I should have let you be on top."

"I was thinking more about the fact that I used muscles I haven't used in…a very long time."

"What muscles would those be? Maybe I could kiss them and make them better."

She laughed softly. "I'm not sure that would actually help, but… Oh."

Her words trailed off on a sigh as he put his suggestion into action.

The power came on a few hours later, as evidenced by the sudden and stark illumination of the stage lights.

Susanna was grateful, of course, to know that the storm had finally passed. But at the same time, she was disappointed that the real world would soon be intruding on her private time with Dean.

Cell service was still out, though, so they each used the landline to check in with their respective moms.

"So when do you think we'll get out of here?" Susanna asked Dean, after all their phone calls had been made and they were watching Maggie with her pups.

"I should think the roads will be cleared within a few hours," he said.

"That soon?" She wasn't sure if she was relieved or disappointed by his response.

"If the town doesn't dig us out, my brothers will—if only to ensure that I'm back at the ranch to do my usual chores tonight."

She managed to laugh at that. "You're probably right. But as much as you guys like to torment one another, you've also got one another's backs."

"Of course," he agreed.

"I always wished I had a sister or a brother, someone who would be in my corner, no matter what."

"Garrett, me, Weston, Crosby and Tyler don't count?" he asked. "And before you remind me yet again that we're not actually your brothers—and after this morning, I should think we're both grateful for *that*—my point is that you can count on us. Anything you need, we'll be there for you. Always."

She nodded, because she knew it was true.

But would Dean ever be able to give her what she really *wanted*?

Dean hadn't been entirely joking when he told her that his brothers would personally plow the roads into town if that was what they needed to do to get to him. But in the end, it was the town that plowed them out. Not that he'd minded being stranded with Susanna. Especially not after they'd discovered ways to pass the time that were much more interesting than conversation.

Of course, he always enjoyed chatting with Susanna, too. She was smart and interesting and they never seemed to run out of things to talk about. But given the choice, he'd take kissing and touching Susanna over talking to her any day of the week. Because as long as they were kissing and touching, he wasn't thinking. Because when he started to think, he inevitably started to wonder about what was going to happen next.

But the question wasn't as scary as the answer. Because what he wanted was to spend every day—and every night—with Susanna by his side. Because with Susanna, he'd experienced a sense of not just contentment but rightness that he'd never known before.

Or maybe he was completely misreading the situation. Maybe making love with Susanna had clouded his brain. Maybe he just needed some space to clear his head and realize that he was making a big deal out of nothing.

Yes, that made more sense, he decided.

But as he headed back to the ranch after dropping her off at home, Dean was forced to admit that his brothers had been right. That one of the reasons—perhaps the main reason—he'd never thought any man she dated was good enough for Susanna was that he wanted her for himself.

And now that he'd had her, he only wanted her again and again.

He managed to push that disquieting realization aside to focus on feeding the cattle and checking their water supply. It was only much later, when the chores were finally done and he was warming up with a hot cup of coffee in the barn, that his mind began to wander again—helped along, in part, by his youngest brother.

"I heard you were stranded at the theater last night," Tyler said.

Dean nodded. "Susanna had car trouble, so I went into town to take her home, but by the time I got there, the storm had intensified so much that we were forced to stay put."

"So after all these years, you finally slept with Susanna."

Tyler was only teasing, of course, referencing the fact that Dean and Susanna had both slept in the same place. Because there was no way he could possibly know what had transpired between them in the dark hours of the morning.

But Dean, whose poker face usually allowed him to come away from card games with more money in his wallet than he'd started with, must have reacted in some way to the remark, because his brother immediately followed up by saying, "Well, damn—you *did* sleep with Susanna."

"Of course I slept with Susanna," he said. "The

power was out and the temperature in the theater dropped, so we huddled together for warmth."

"Huddled together for warmth, huh?" Tyler said, clearly not buying his explanation.

"Who was huddled together for warmth?" Crosby asked, walking into the room—and the middle of their conversation.

"Dean and Susanna," Tyler said, as Weston came in next and made his way to the coffeepot.

"Oh, yeah. I heard you went into town to rescue Susanna last night—and ended up needing to be rescued yourself." Weston chuckled, obviously amused by his own interpretation of the situation.

"I didn't need to be rescued," Dean denied. "We just had to wait for the storm to pass and the roads to be cleared."

"Well, I'm sure Susanna was grateful you were there," Crosby said.

"It's a good thing we were both there," Dean said, and proceeded to tell his brothers about Maggie's arrival at the theater, followed soon after by the arrival of her eight puppies.

"Daphne's going to be busy at Happy Hearts," Garrett noted, "with everyone traipsing through to see the puppies."

"And wanting to take one home."

"Or take all of them home," Dean said. "Those pups are seriously adorable."

"Puppies are also a lot of work," Crosby said.

"Almost as much as human babies," Tyler—the voice of experience—chimed in.

"Still, we could use a dog around here again," Garrett mused. "It's been a few years since Bandit crossed the rainbow bridge."

Dean exhaled a quiet sigh of relief that he'd managed to sidetrack his brothers from their questions about his night with Susanna by sharing the news about Maggie's puppies.

Or at least most of his brothers.

"That was a good distraction," Tyler noted, after Garrett, Weston and Crosby had gone. "But don't think I don't know you didn't want to talk about Susanna."

"I didn't not want to talk about Susanna," he denied. "I just didn't have anything to say."

"Why don't I believe you?"

He shrugged. "Because you're inherently suspicious?"

His brother shook his head. "She's not the type of woman who has casual relationships, and I guarantee, if something happened between the two of you last night, it meant a lot more to Susanna than it did to you."

"Why are we even having this conversation?"

"Because I'm looking out for her as any brother would look out for his sister."

"But she's not your sister—or mine."

And thank God for that! The thought sprang immediately to mind along with memories of their naked lovemaking earlier that morning.

"That's certainly a different tune than the one you were singing not even two weeks ago," Tyler mused.

Which was an undeniable truth. But a lot had changed in those two weeks—or, more specifically, in the last two days.

"I'm going to ride out and check the fence to see how much damage was done by the storm," he decided. Because even if he couldn't escape his own introspection, he could at least earn a reprieve from his brother's questions.

"Just…be careful," Tyler said.

"It's sweet of you to worry, but I've been riding fence for a lot of years. I'll be fine."

His brother rolled his eyes. "I meant be careful with Susanna."

Dean's only response to that was to walk out.

After the storm had passed and the residents of Bronco had dug themselves out from under all the snow, the cast and crew only had one day left to rehearse in advance of opening night. Susanna worried that the lost time would be evident onstage, and there were a few glitches, though they didn't seem to faze Chuck at all. In fact, he seemed relieved that there were snags during the dress rehearsal—one of which was being unable to find the dress that Susanna was supposed to wear in the final scene!—no doubt believing the superstition that a bad dress rehearsal was a good omen for a successful opening.

After Chuck told them all to go home and get some rest so that they'd ready to bring the house down the following night, a woman hurried down the center aisle of the theater and waved to get Avery's attention.

Susanna didn't give the woman any more than a passing thought until she'd finished going over some notes with Marty and was ready to leave—already mentally scanning the contents of her closet for anything suitable that might stand in for the missing dress the following night—when Avery said, "Do you have a minute?"

"Sure," she agreed. "What's up?"

"I want to show you something," Avery said, and led the way to the women's dressing room where she gestured with a flourish to the BH Couture garment bag hanging from a hook.

"What is it?" Susanna asked.

"Open it and see," Avery urged, fairly dancing with excitement.

Susanna unzipped the bag, her own anticipation shifting to confusion. "It's my dress."

"It's your dress," Avery confirmed.

"I don't understand. Why is my dress in a bag from BH Couture?"

"Have you ever heard the expression 'It's better to ask forgiveness than permission'?"

She nodded.

"Well, I hope you'll forgive me if I overstepped,

but my mom is a seamstress at BH Couture—and an absolute wizard with a needle and thread. So I asked her to take your size ten dress and make it a size twelve."

"And she did?" Susanna was almost afraid to hope.

The other woman nodded.

She examined the side seams, where narrow panels of matching fabric had been sewn in so perfectly that, even on close inspection, they were almost invisible. "She does amazing work."

"She does," Avery agreed. "Now go ahead—try it on."

She eagerly shed her clothes and stepped into the dress.

"Can you zip me?"

"Of course."

The zipper closed without any difficulty and when Susanna dared to lift her gaze to the mirror, she couldn't help but smile. She turned to examine her reflection from the side, confirming that there was no pinching of fabric or pulling of seams. "It looks good."

"It looks great," Avery said. "*You* look great."

"I don't know what to say," Susanna admitted. "'Thank you' seems so inadequate."

"Does that mean I'm forgiven?"

"You're forgiven," she confirmed. "And I'm so grateful. This is one of the kindest things anyone has ever done for me."

"If that's true, then you need to get some new friends," Avery told her, making Susanna laugh.

And then she gave her new friend a hug.

"I'm so glad you're happy with the alterations," Avery said, as they walked out of the theater together. "And just a little bit disappointed that Irene's daughter-in-law went into labor early so she won't be here tomorrow night to see how absolutely fabulous you'll look."

Susanna was happy, too.

Almost happy enough to forget that she hadn't seen or heard from Dean in almost two days. Not since he'd dropped her off at home after the night they'd been stranded together at the theater.

It was partly her fault. She'd booked those days off work so that she could dedicate her time to rehearsals and all the other little tasks she needed to take care of in preparation for opening night.

But why hadn't he called? Or at least sent a text message?

Had their night together meant nothing to him?

Or had she made the mistake in letting it mean too much to her?

He should call her.

Or at least text.

Dean was accustomed to seeing Susanna almost every day, and it felt strange to look into her office at Abernathy Meats and not see her sitting behind the desk.

It felt stranger still to realize how much he missed not seeing her there.

To realize that a day without Susanna was like a day without sunshine.

And yeah, the sentiment was both cliché and pathetic, but it was also true. Her mere presence was enough to brighten the offices—and lift his mood.

But maybe it was good that she'd taken a couple days off. They hadn't really had a chance to talk after the night they'd spent together at the theater, and he suspected that they both needed some time to figure things out.

He knew for sure that he did.

Because making love with Susanna had been an incredible experience and he certainly wasn't opposed to the idea of getting naked with her again. But then what?

He didn't have a great track record with relationships. Though he prided himself on treating women well, he wasn't known for sharing his thoughts and feelings. More than once, Whitney had remarked that she should have been a dental assistant, because getting him to talk was like pulling teeth. He didn't think he was *that* bad, but it was true that he'd never felt particularly comfortable opening up to her. Maybe because what he most needed to open up about was his concerns about their relationship, and he'd known that she didn't want to hear them.

The funny thing was, he'd never had any trouble talking to Susanna about anything. But this was different, because they'd had sex, and sex—even really great sex—changed everything.

And while his body was in favor of having really great sex with her again and again, his mind and his heart were wary. Because it hadn't just been sex; it had been *sex with Susanna*, who wasn't only a friend and an employee of Abernathy Meats, but practically a member of the family.

He'd always known that his parents loved her like a daughter, but now that he knew a little bit more about her family history, he understood how much that relationship meant to her, too. And the last thing he ever wanted to do was mess up that relationship— if it wasn't already too late.

So yeah, he had some things to figure out—and he hoped like hell that he'd figure them out before tomorrow night, when he'd be sitting in the front row for the opening of her play.

"I wasn't sure if the recent storm would keep people away, but apparently it's a packed house," Marty said, joining Susanna in the backstage area on opening night.

"How do you know?"

"Brian's been texting me updates from the front row."

"People were probably eager to get out after being shut in for the better part of two days," Susanna surmised.

"Or they heard that Winona Cobbs predicted our

show was going to be the highlight of the holiday season."

"Did she say that?" Susanna lifted a hand to her mouth, to nibble on the corner of her thumbnail. She wasn't usually a nail-biter, but when she was really nervous, that one thumbnail paid the price. "Did you actually go to see her?"

Marty caught her wrist and pulled her hand away. "Would it make you feel better if I said that I did?"

"Probably not," she admitted.

He linked their fingers together and gave hers a reassuring squeeze.

"Opening night is the one night when my nerves manage to outweigh my excitement," she confided.

"You know you're going to be great, right? Just like you've been at every rehearsal for the past two weeks."

She managed a smile. "I appreciate your vote of confidence."

"And I'm going to be great, too, right?" he asked.

"You know you're the real star of the show— every woman in the audience tonight is going to fall a little bit in love with you."

"In love with Noel, you mean."

"Because on that stage, you are Noel," she reminded him.

"And Noel knows the heart of the woman he loves, so she should tell him what's really bothering her," he urged.

"Nothing," she said.

"He also knows when she's lying to him," Marty

pointed out. "Just like I know when you're being less than truthful with me."

"I'm not," she insisted. "Because I'm not going to let anything bother me. Tonight I am focused on this play."

"You'll tell me tomorrow?"

She managed a smile. "I'll tell you tomorrow."

He kissed her forehead. "Okay, let's go out there and break a leg."

She was good, Dean acknowledged, as he watched Susanna onstage. Really good.

Of course, it wasn't the first time he'd seen her perform, and he'd always admired her ability to seemingly become a different person onstage. But this time, she wasn't just playing a character, she'd created the character. In fact, she'd created all of the characters onstage and the storyline that brought them together.

Marty was good, too, Dean had to admit, impressed by his depiction of the character as he transformed Noel from Holly's clueless friend to finally realizing that he was in love with her.

The parallel romance of Holly's friend, Joy, and Noel's friend, Jack, added interest and depth to the story, with frequent appearances by Star adding the comic relief. The climax played out as Susanna had described, with Noel interrupting what he thought was Jack's proposal to Holly and ultimately confessing his own feelings and asking her to marry him.

"I don't have a ring yet," Noel said. "But I have this—a symbol of my heart, which belongs to you. For now and forever."

Holly held up the heart-shaped ornament he gave her to admire it in the light—and so the audience could see it. "It's perfect."

Together they hung the ornament on the tree, then Noel drew Holly into his arms for a kiss.

Dean applauded along with everyone else in the theater, though he wasn't happy to see Susanna in the arms of—and kissing—the other man. True, he'd been given a heads-up that there would be a kiss between the two main characters at the end of the show, but that knowledge hadn't prepared him for the uncomfortable feeling churning in his gut as he watched it play out onstage and found himself wondering how many times they'd practiced that final scene.

As the light on the couple started to fade, the light on the Christmas tree grew brighter, illuminating the figure in the red suit who was pulling presents out of his sack and setting them under the tree.

Chants of "Santa! Santa!" came from young members of the audience, growing in volume and excitement.

The jolly elf turned around then and offered his fans a wave and a wink, then the stage went dark.

"The sound of applause never gets old, does it?" Marty said, linking his hand with Susanna's to face the audience and take a bow.

"Never," Susanna agreed, smiling as her eyes searched the front row of mostly familiar faces.

When the curtain calls were finished, friends and family were allowed backstage to visit with the cast and crew. Joyce and Ted were there, as was Dean with his parents and Garrett and Weston. Crosby had already told Susanna that he and Victoria had tickets for Friday night, and Tyler and Callie were planning to attend Saturday's performance while his parents babysat Maeve.

Susanna accepted hugs and flowers—red roses from her mom, pink from Hutch and Hannah, and yellow (the color of friendship!) from Dean, Garrett and Weston. She'd planned to ask Dean to stick around after everyone else had gone, but he slipped out with his brothers, just as Marty's husband clapped his hands together to draw everyone's attention, and the opportunity was lost.

She shook off her disappointment and focused on Brian.

"A successful opening night should be celebrated," he announced to the gathering. "And it happens that we've got several bottles of champagne at our place—"

Whatever he intended to say after that was drowned out by a chorus of cheers, forcing him to pause with a grin.

"I thought we were saving those for a special occasion," Marty protested, when everyone had quieted down.

"This *is* a special occasion," Brian pointed out,

then turned to the crowd again. "As I was saying, we've got champagne and snacks—"

More cheers.

"You better not plan on serving my imported Gruyère," Marty grumbled.

Brian ignored him.

"—for anyone who would like to join us at 39 White Oak Drive," he finished.

There was no way Susanna was going to refuse the invitation, or resist the opportunity to take a peek at their new home, and she happily hitched a ride with the hosts of the impromptu party.

She helped Marty and Brian set out the snacks (including the Gruyère) and pour champagne (the real stuff!), then mingled with the cast and crew and their friends/partners/spouses. As she did so, she found herself pondering Dean's recent behavior.

In her mind, the night they'd spent together had changed everything. They were no longer just friends, but lovers, and she'd been excited to contemplate their future together.

But now that she thought about it, he hadn't even tried to kiss her goodbye when he'd dropped her off at home after the snowstorm. Of course, Susanna's mother had been standing at the window, obviously watching for their arrival, and in the moment, she'd appreciated being spared the hundred and one questions Joyce would have asked if she'd caught even a glimpse of something between them.

But perhaps Dean had seen her mother in the window and been grateful for an excuse to say a quick goodbye and be on his way.

Did he regret what had happened between them?

Was she just his latest hookup?

The possibility made her heart ache, but it also steeled her resolve.

For too many years, she'd been steady and dependable Susanna Henry, content to wait in the wings and hope that the man she loved might one day love her back.

Now, in the company of so many happy couples, she felt inspired to take her future in her own hands and go get her man.

Chapter Fourteen

Three days after the opening of *A Christmas Wish*—and six days after the night Susanna and Dean had spent together in the theater—she was growing increasingly frustrated by scheduling conflicts that kept both Dean and her busy in different places so that they didn't have any time alone together. But today was the fifth annual Christmas at the Farm and Susanna had managed to persuade an obviously reluctant Dean to go with her to the Happy Hearts open house.

Their easy conversation on the way to the farm assuaged some of the doubts that had been swirling in her mind. And when Dean offered his hand to help her out of his truck, she was happy to continue to hold on to it as they made their way around the property, walking along fences draped with evergreen boughs decorated with twinkling lights and red velvet bows, and hearing the stories of Gretel the dairy cow and Winnie the sheep and Tiny Tim the not-at-all-tiny potbellied pig.

There was no admission charged to attend the open house, but Daphne had cleverly ensured there were numerous opportunities for visitors to make donations in support of the care and rehabilitation of the animals who resided at Happy Hearts.

"We didn't really have a chance to talk after the show on Wednesday," she said to Dean, as they wandered past a pair of roughhousing goats.

"You were basking in the glory of your fans—and rightfully so," he told her. "I don't think I ever before realized how completely you become your character when you're onstage. Watching you and Marty—you were Holly and Noel, and I had absolutely no doubt that you were meant to be together."

"That's high praise," she said. "Thank you."

"But I realized something else, too," he told her.

"What's that?"

"I can't believe I'm saying this but...your talents are wasted here. You should be on a bigger stage in front of a bigger audience."

"I happen to enjoy performing in community theater."

"There was a time when you wanted more," he reminded her.

"When I was seventeen."

"You're saying you don't want more now?" he asked, sounding dubious.

Of course, she wanted more for her life. She wanted a husband and children. A family of her own. But her involvement in community theater was exactly what she needed to satisfy her artistic dreams.

"You're only twenty-five," he continued. "It can't

be too late to follow your dreams to Los Angeles or New York—to show the world what you're capable of."

Ordinarily she would be flattered that someone—anyone—believed she might have the talent required to make it in either of those cities. But such encouragement from Dean now—mere days after they'd made love, when they'd shared such a profound physical connection she'd been certain he must have real feelings for her—made her uneasy.

She turned to look at him and cautiously asked, "Where is this coming from?"

"I'm just trying to be supportive," he said. "Like any friend should be."

And it wasn't her imagination that he'd emphasized the word *friend*.

Obviously he was trying to put their relationship firmly back into the platonic zone and had been since they'd left the theater after the storm. The signs had all been there—she'd just refused to read them.

Until now.

Until he'd hit her over the head with the fact that he didn't see a future for them together.

How could she have been so foolish as to think he might actually want a relationship with her?

Just because their lovemaking had totally rocked her world didn't mean it had any impact on his.

When the storm had finally passed, he'd been chomping at the bit to leave the theater. Which she understood. She knew there was always a lot of work to be done at the ranch—probably even more than usual in the aftermath of the storm—and it was natural that he'd feel guilty about not being there to pull his weight. Even if his absence was through no fault of his own.

And while he'd shown up at the theater for opening night, he hadn't stuck around any longer than absolutely necessary afterward. And even when she'd broached the idea of attending the open house together, he'd only acquiesced after she'd reminded him that she didn't have any way of getting there on her own, because her vehicle was still with her mechanic. Because he was too nice to leave her stranded.

Because he was her *friend*.

And suddenly, spending the day with him was the last thing she wanted to do.

Barely a minute after that, Dean spotted a friend and dropped Susanna's hand to lift his own in a wave.

Apparently he didn't want his friend to see them holding hands and assume—obviously mistakenly—that they were together.

Susanna took the hint and tucked both of her hands into the pockets of her coat as Dean's friend approached.

"Hey, Steve." The two men shook hands. "How are you doing?"

"I'm surprised to see you here," the other man—Steve—replied to Dean's question. "I would have guessed that ranchers were persona non grata around here."

"So now you're a lawyer and a comedian?"

Steve grinned. "And soon to be a cat owner, apparently. My wife and daughters raced ahead to the adoption center, their hearts set on adding a four-legged friend to our family before the holidays."

"How old are the twins now?" Dean asked.

"Just turned five."

"Wow."

"So what's going on with you?" Steve asked, his gaze sliding over to Susanna. "Last time I saw you, you'd just gotten engaged."

"Um, yeah. That didn't work out," Dean said.

"Oh." The other man looked at Susanna again and shrugged. "This awkward moment is brought to you by an obviously out-of-touch friend of Dean's from high school."

His tone was easy and friendly, so Susanna smiled and offered her hand. "I'm Susanna Henry."

Steve snapped his fingers. "Now I know why you look familiar," he said. "We saw *A Christmas Wish* Wednesday night. It was wonderful."

"I'm glad you enjoyed it."

"So you're an actor."

"Part-time," she said.

"Susanna is also the office manager at Abernathy Meats," Dean chimed in. "And a friend."

Steve heard his phone ping with a message and pulled it out of his pocket to glance at the screen.

"Apparently I better hurry up or we're going to end up with two cats." He tucked his phone away again. "Well, it was good to see you again, Dean. And really nice to meet you, Susanna."

"You, too," she said. "Good luck with the cats."

"Cat," he said, emphasizing the singular.

She just smiled as he hurried off in the direction of the adoption shelter, but her smile quickly faded.

"Well, that was an eye opener," she said to Dean, when his friend was out of earshot.

"What?"

"I didn't realize that you viewed me, first and foremost, as an employee of Abernathy Meats."

"What are you talking about?"

"You introduced me to Steve as the office manager."

"Well, you are the office manager," he pointed out.

"And then you tacked on the fact that we were friends, as if it was an afterthought."

"I didn't mean it like that," he said.

"How did you mean it?" she challenged.

"I just don't like everyone knowing my personal business."

"You mean you don't want everyone—or maybe *anyone*—to know that we slept together."

"Do *you* want everyone to know that we slept together?" he challenged.

"I'm not ashamed of the fact," she said pointedly.

"Is that what you think—that I'm ashamed of what happened between us?"

"I get it," she said, lifting her shoulder in a hopefully nonchalant shrug that would belie the fact that her heart was breaking. "I'm not at all your usual type. I just happened to be there, not just willing but eager, and in the light of day—or at least by the next day—you realized that it was a mistake."

"That isn't at all what happened," he denied.

"Actually, that's *exactly* what happened," she countered. "I practically threw myself at you. All you did was catch."

"I kissed you first," he pointed out.

It was true.

And then he'd immediately backpedaled.

He'd said no.

Until early the next morning, when he'd awakened in a state of arousal with a willing woman in his arms.

The sex had been amazing, so she couldn't regret that. Her mistake had been in giving him not only her body but also her heart.

She glanced at the display on her Fitbit. "I need to go home and get ready for tonight."

"It's not even two o'clock," he pointed out. "And we haven't seen Maggie yet."

"I forgot that I have to fix something…the hem… on my dress."

"Isn't there someone who takes care of wardrobe issues?"

"Our costume designer isn't going to be there to-night. Her daughter-in-law just had a baby, so she's in Nebraska."

She was saying too much and talking too fast, but Susanna was afraid that if she stopped talking she'd start crying—and there was no way she was going to let Dean see her cry.

Not again.

And definitely not over him.

"But if you're not ready to go, I can give my mom a call and ask her to pick me up," she continued. "She's not working today, so I'm sure she wouldn't mind."

He was watching her closely, as if he knew there was more going on than she was telling him, so maybe he wasn't completely clueless after all.

"I'm ready to go," he finally said.

"Okay. Great." She forced a smile. "Let's go."

He drove most of the way in silence, the only sound in the cab of his truck being the Christmas carols that played on the radio.

"Is everything okay?" he asked, as they neared her house. "You seem preoccupied."

"I've just got a lot on my mind," she said.

"Anything you want to talk about?"

"Just theater stuff. Not anything that would interest you," she assured him.

"Actually, I was fascinated by all the stuff you told me the night we were stranded at the theater."

And there it was—the one topic, above all others,

that she'd been hoping to avoid. The one thing she didn't even want to think about right now.

Because she couldn't remember what had happened that night without wanting him all over again, and he'd made it painfully clear that he didn't want her at all.

As soon as he pulled into the driveway, before he'd even shifted into Park, Susanna had unlatched her seat belt and was opening the door to hop out.

"Susanna—wait," he urged.

She shook her head, fighting the tears that burned the back of her eyes. "I really can't. I've got a lot to do before tonight."

Then she slammed the door and hurried into the house, not giving him a chance to follow.

Not giving him a chance to *not* kiss her.

He'd screwed up. Big-time.

Dean wasn't entirely sure what he'd done, but he knew that he'd hurt Susanna—and that was the absolute last thing he ever wanted to do.

So he went back to the ranch and climbed up to the hayloft, rearranging bags of feed because all the usual chores were done but he needed to sweat out his frustration. And then, when he'd finished there, he went down to the tack room to grab a cup of coffee.

"So how was the play?" Tyler asked, looking up from the saddle he was oiling. "Me and Callie are going tonight and I want to know what to expect."

"It was good," Dean told him.

"Are you talking about Susanna's play?" Crosby asked, as he and Garrett joined them in the tack room.

Tyler nodded.

"It's a definite improvement over last year's *Nutcracker*," Garrett said.

"You mean the ballerina who couldn't dance?" Tyler shuddered at the memory. "So tell me what *The Christmas Wish* is about."

Garrett and Crosby shared a glance and smirked.

"It's about a guy who's totally oblivious to the fact that the girl he treats as a buddy is his perfect match," Crosby finally said.

"Like Dean and Susanna?" Tyler guessed.

Garrett snapped his fingers together. "Exactly."

Dean shook his head. "You guys really are idiots."

"Until another man starts to show an interest in the girl," Crosby continued.

"Like Marty?" Tyler prompted.

Garrett nodded. "Our brother has been bent out of shape since Susanna started spending time with Marty."

"He doesn't like the fact that Roger's been hanging out with her, too," Crosby noted.

"I just don't think either of them is the right guy for her," Dean said, feeling distinctly uncomfortable with the direction of this conversation.

"So who do you think would be the right guy for her?" Crosby challenged.

He shrugged. "Someone who appreciates all of her wonderful qualities," he said. "Her kindness and generosity. Her quick sense of humor. The way her eyes sparkle when she smiles."

"Hmm," Tyler mused.

Crosby nodded. "You might think he was actually describing himself."

"An argument could be made," Garrett agreed.

He scowled. "I don't have a romantic interest in Susanna." Which was a total lie, but Dean had no intention of admitting the truth and giving his brothers more ammunition to use against him.

"He just wants to get in her pants, but he's—"

Dean didn't consciously act, but suddenly he'd grabbed Crosby by the front of his shirt and shoved him back against the wall. "What the hell's wrong with you?"

His brother recovered quickly from the shock of Dean's action and his lips curved in a slow, smug smile. "I don't think I'm the one who has a problem."

"You will if I ever hear you talk about Susanna that way again," he promised.

"I'm not sure what I said that's so offensive. She's an attractive woman…"

Dean growled. He actually growled—a feral sound that rumbled low in his throat. "Don't say another word about her pants."

"She did look great in that dress she wore on-stage," Garrett remarked, apparently unable to resist adding fuel to the fire that burned in Dean's gut. "Who knew she had legs like that?"

He let go of Crosby and turned to his older brother.

Garrett held up his hands in a gesture of surrender. "I'm just sayin'."

"You shouldn't be *sayin'* anything about Susanna," Dean told him.

"Come on," Tyler said, attempting to play peacemaker. "It's one thing to taunt a guy about a woman he met in a bar. It's another thing to tease him about the woman he loves."

Dean opened his mouth to refute the claim, then staggered back a step as he considered that there might be some truth to his brother's words.

There was no denying that he cared about Susanna.

He always had.

It was only more recently that he'd acknowledged his attraction to her, though he'd successfully managed to ignore it—until the night they were stranded together in the theater.

But love?

Was it possible?

Could he be in love with Susanna?

He dumped the mug of coffee he'd only recently poured.

He was going to need something a lot stronger.

Susanna was almost always the first one at the theater, so she was surprised to walk into the dressing room Saturday afternoon and find that Liz was already there.

"You're here early today," she remarked.

"I had an appointment in town this afternoon, so I came here directly after."

"Everything okay?"

"I'm not sure," Liz confided. "I did something today that I didn't think I'd ever do."

"What's that?" Susanna asked, because it seemed obvious that the other woman wanted to tell her.

"I went to Wisdom by Winona."

"You're a braver woman than I."

"I don't know if I was feeling brave or just desperate for advice," Liz admitted.

"Was Winona helpful?"

"I hope so."

"That's good, then, I guess," Susanna said.

"She said that my fear of rejection is holding me back from going after what I want," the other woman confided.

"Nobody wants to be rejected," she agreed.

"And she suggested that I follow my heart."

The exact same advice was written on an inspirational poster hanging in the public library, available to all free of charge.

"So I've decided to ask Roger if he wants to grab a drink after the show tonight," Liz continued.

"He'd be a fool to say no."

The other woman offered a tentative smile. "I appreciate you saying so. Of course, I've known a lot of men who were fools, so I'm not getting my hopes up, but I'm going to ask anyway."

More proof that Liz was a braver woman than Susanna, who'd lied to Dean about needing to fix her costume rather than tell him the truth about her feelings.

"Anyway, I just thought I should tell you about my plans because, well, Avery said that there wasn't anything going on between you and Roger, but I wanted to be sure."

"There's nothing going on between me and Roger," she confirmed.

"Then I guess there's no reason that I shouldn't do this," Liz said.

"None at all," Susanna agreed. "And if he *is* foolish enough to say no, I'll take you out for a drink to commiserate about the idiocy of men."

Liz smiled then. "I'd like that. I mean, I hope Roger says yes so it doesn't happen, but it would be nice to hang out and chat."

Susanna managed to smile back, grateful that her conversation with Liz had taken her mind off Dean—at least for a few minutes.

Chapter Fifteen

"Susanna, you've got a visitor."

Her heart leaped with foolish hope, quickly extinguished when she turned to see Alicia Krecji standing in the doorway of the women's dressing room.

"I hope you don't mind that I came backstage," Alicia said.

"Of course not," Susanna said, because she was always happy to welcome visitors to the other side of the curtain and she wasn't going to treat Alicia any differently. "I just didn't realize you were even in town. I mean, I'd heard you were back in Bronco, but I figured you'd be in Nebraska now."

"I'm excited to meet my new niece," Alicia said. "But not so excited that I wanted to drive nine hours in a car with my mom to get there—and then another nine hours back again."

"I've got a mom, too," Susanna said sympathetically.

"Not like mine."

And thank God for that.

But, of course, Susanna kept that sentiment to herself.

"Anyway, I decided to take advantage of her being

out of town to enjoy your play, minus her commentary," Alicia continued. "And it was wonderful. Not that I was the least bit surprised. You always were an incredibly talented actor. But the script, too, was fabulous."

"Thank you."

"Did you know that I read for a part?"

"Not until recently," Susanna told her.

"Did Marty tell you how awful I was? No, don't answer that," she said. "I'm not sure I want to know. It's been a long time since I was onstage, and although I'd like to get back to it, I'm not looking for any starring roles. I was actually hoping to play Joy—or even Star, when I saw the cast list. But my mom pushed me to audition for the role of Holly.

"And I'm only telling you that now so that you can keep me in mind, perhaps, when you write your next script. I can be the heroine's former-competitor-turned-friend."

"As it happens, I am working on a new script," Susanna confided.

"I have no doubt we'll be seeing a lot more Susanna Henry productions in the future," Alicia said.

"Susanna—oh," Marty halted in midstride just inside the doorway. "I didn't realize you had a visitor."

"I was just leaving," Alicia said. "Congrats again, to both of you, on your fabulous performances tonight."

"Thank you," Susanna and Marty responded in unison.

"So...was that awkward?" Marty asked cautiously, after Alicia had gone.

"Actually, no," Susanna told him.

Over the years, she'd managed to forget that she and Alicia used to be friends, before they started competing for the same roles. And she was pleased to think that they might find their way back to being friends again.

"Well, that's good, then," he said.

She nodded. "So what did you need?"

"I just wanted to catch you before you left, because we haven't had a chance to talk about whatever's been bothering you."

"Why do you think something's bothering me? I didn't miss any of my cues or stumble over any of my lines," she said, perhaps a little defensively.

"No, you didn't," he agreed. "You nailed your performance, as you do every night."

"Then what makes you think there's a problem?"

"The fact that your eyes weren't sparkling the way they usually do when you're onstage."

"It's been a busy few weeks—I'm just tired."

He nodded. "That sounded pretty convincing—and maybe it's even true, but it's not the whole truth."

"It's my story and I'm sticking to it," she said.

"Okay, then," he said, sounding wounded. "I guess I was mistaken in thinking we were friends."

Susanna caught his arm as he started to turn away. "No, you weren't mistaken. The problem is that *I* obviously don't understand what it means to be friends."

"Do you want to explain that?"

"Maybe." She sighed. "But once I start talking, I might not be able to stop."

"In that case, let's get out of here and go grab a drink."

Marty took her to Doug's, a hole-in-the-wall bar in Bronco Valley with a reputation for cold beer and not much else.

She glanced down at her jeggings and green Christmas sweater. "I don't know that I'm dressed appropriately for a fancy place like this," she joked, as she followed her costar into the nondescript building.

"I was going to say something but—" Marty shrugged "—most of the regulars here won't judge."

"I feel so much better now."

The easy smile died on her lips when she spotted a familiar figure over Marty's shoulder.

She must have made some kind of sound, because he turned to look at her, then followed the direction of her gaze to where Dean was seated across from his brother Garrett.

"Damn," Marty muttered. "I didn't think we'd run into any Abernathys here."

Susanna could understand why he'd made that assumption. Because most of the wealthy ranching families in Bronco belonged to The Association, where they could socialize with their own kind and not have to worry about rubbing elbows with the common folk while they sipped their thirty-year-old whiskey.

"Do you want to go somewhere else?" he asked her now.

"Of course not," she lied. "This is fine."

"Translation: of course, I do, but there's no way I'm going to give him the satisfaction of knowing that I walked out because I didn't want to see him."

"You really are intuitive, aren't you?" she murmured.

"It's only one of my many talents," he said immodestly, as he led her to a table as far away as possible from Dean and Garrett.

Not as far away as she would have liked, but she appreciated the effort.

"Do you want something to eat?" Marty asked. "I'm always starving after a performance."

Susanna usually was, too, but seeing Dean here had effectively killed her appetite. "I didn't think this place was known for its food."

"Spoken by someone who has never tried Doug's chili cheese nachos," he said.

As if on cue, a server appeared at their table. "What can I get for ya?"

Susanna was usually a wine drinker, and although she wasn't a wine snob, she was a little put off by the vague "house white" and "house red" descriptions.

"I'll have a light beer," she said. "Whatever you have on tap."

The server shifted her attention to Marty.

"I'll have a Coke and the nachos. Extra sour cream."

"A Coke?" Susanna said, when the server had gone.

He shrugged. "What can I say? I'm feeling a little reckless tonight."

"What do you order when you're not feeling reckless?"

"Diet Coke."

She chuckled at that.

"There it is…almost…nope, it's gone again."

"What are you talking about?"

"Your missing sparkle."

She dropped her gaze and looked away. "So…did you and Brian decide what you're doing for Christmas?"

"You're deflecting," Marty said accusingly.

"No, I'm showing an interest in my friend's life."

"In that case, I'll tell you that we're spending it here, in our new home, and leaving for Florida on the twenty-seventh."

Susanna smiled. "And how did you come to that decision?"

"It was actually Brian's idea," he confided. "After you and I talked in your office, I had every intention of broaching the topic with him over dinner that night, but he brought up the subject before I could. He said as happy as he was that his parents wanted to spend time with us over the holidays, he didn't want to spend our first Christmas in our new home somewhere other than our new home."

"Sounds like you guys are perfectly in sync with what you want—and each other."

"Yeah, I'm a lucky guy," Marty said, then he shook his head. "No, he's a lucky guy."

She laughed. "I think you're both lucky."

"We are," he agreed with a smile. "And although my mother-in-law was disappointed to learn that we won't be with them on Christmas morning, she seemed happy enough to know that we'll be there for New Year's."

"A perfect compromise."

Marty nodded, then waited until their drinks had been delivered before he said, "Now tell me what happened with your cowboy."

This time, she didn't hesitate or hedge. "We had sex, and it was everything I'd always hoped it would be except that now he wants to pretend it never happened. Or maybe he wishes it never happened."

"Then he really is an idiot," Marty said.

"You won't get any argument from me there," she assured him.

"And you can do better than an idiot."

She tried to smile again, and gave up when she felt her lips tremble rather than curve.

"Unfortunately, that doesn't stop you from wanting the idiot, does it?" he murmured sympathetically.

"Not yet, but I'm working on it."

"Confession time," Marty said. "I've had some experience with the whole why-is-he-being-such-an-idiot stage of a relationship."

"With Brian?" she guessed.

He nodded.

"What did he do?"

"Actually, it wasn't him—it was me." Marty swallowed a mouthful of cola. "I was still living in New York at the time and, when he came to visit me, we packed a picnic and went to Central Park. And while we were eating peanut butter and jelly sandwiches and drinking cheap wine, I realized that I had never been as happy as I was in that moment. With Brian.

"And he must have felt the same way, because he told me that he loved me. And… I panicked."

"What did you do?" she asked.

"I told him that we should take a break from our relationship and see other people. Just for six months. Just to be sure."

"How did he respond?"

"He said no deal. If I needed six months to date other people to know that we were meant to be together, then I wasn't the man he thought I was. And then he left."

"Tough love," she murmured.

"And I let him go, because I wasn't just an idiot, I was proud and stubborn and no way was I going to give in to an ultimatum."

"What happened next?"

"Three hours later, I tracked him down at the airport and begged him to forgive me."

"Obviously he did."

"He made me grovel," Marty admitted. "But yeah, in the end, he forgave me. So you see, there is hope that your idiot cowboy will come around."

But Susanna wasn't optimistic.

"He's had eight years to come around," she pointed out.

"Eight years," her costar echoed, surprised. "But…you were only a teenager eight years ago."

She nodded. "Unfortunately, Dean still sees me that way. Well, most of the time," she amended, as their lovemaking played out in her mind like a movie reel. It had been replaying at all times and every day since the night they'd spent together, and that was why she'd finally arrived at her decision.

She wasn't planning to run off to California or New York as Dean had suggested, but she'd finally realized that she couldn't continue working at Abernathy Meats and seeing him every day. Not if she had any hope of getting over him.

Making love with Dean had been even more incredible than she'd imagined, but reality had finally burst her fairy-tale bubble. Because Dean didn't want a future with her. He didn't even want a day after with her. And if she was ever going to find someone with whom to share her life, she had to let go of her illusions about the handsome cowboy once and for all.

"But more important," she continued, "it's time

for me to stop hoping and dreaming and move on with my life."

"It sounds like you've already got a plan," Marty noted.

She nodded. "And the first step is looking for a new job."

"In Bronco?"

Now she shook her head. "So long as there's the possibility of seeing Dean every day, I'm never going to get over him."

"Out of sight, out of mind?" he said dubiously.

"That's the idea," she said, holding up her hand to show her fingers were crossed.

"You know there's another old saying, don't you?" He answered his own question without giving her a chance to do so. "Absence makes the heart grow fonder."

"I know," she acknowledged. "But I don't mind having fond memories…as long as I'm moving forward with my life."

"You'll come back to visit, though," he said, a question more than a statement.

"Of course. After all, my mom is still going to be living here. Although maybe she'll be living with Ted before too long."

"I meant come back to visit me," Marty clarified.

"Absolutely," Susanna promised, and this time her smile came more easily.

Dean had been in a lousy mood after he dropped Susanna off at home following their very brief visit to Happy Hearts. Because he knew that there was something off with her, and though he wasn't sure what that something was, he was pretty sure that he was the cause of it.

Garrett had picked up on his mood and suggested that they go into town for a beer "to get your mind off whatever the hell has put you in such a mood."

Seeing Susanna show up at Doug's with her co-star had done nothing to improve his disposition.

"Well, at least now I know what caused your lousy mood," Garrett remarked.

Dean yanked his gaze away from Susanna's table. "What?"

"Something happen between the two of you?" his brother pressed.

"Who?" he asked, feigning a nonchalance he wasn't even close to feeling.

Garrett shook his head. "If you don't want to talk about it, just say you don't want to talk about it."

"I don't want to talk about it." He swallowed a mouthful of beer and then immediately contradicted his own claim by saying, "But dammit…what is she doing here with him?"

"Looks like they're having a drink—and nachos," his brother remarked as the server delivered a heaping plate of chips smothered in chili and cheese to the table where Susanna and Marty were seated.

"Nachos are carbs," Dean said, frowning. "She said she's trying to cut down on carbs."

"Why?" Garrett asked.

He shrugged, not wanting to get into a conversation with his brother about Susanna's curves and draw Garrett's attention to her tempting shape.

"So are we talking about it or not talking about it?" his brother prompted when Dean remained silent.

"You mean about the fact that Susanna is here with Marty less than a week after we spent the night together?"

"You were stranded together in the middle of a blizzard," Garrett noted. "Sometimes things happen in situations like that—it doesn't have to be a big deal."

Except that it was a big deal—at least to Dean.

But maybe it hadn't meant anything to her.

"How could it not mean anything to her?"

"So we're talking about it," Garrett noted.

"Barely a week ago, she was out with Roger. Now it's Marty."

"You have a problem with Susanna socializing with other members of the cast?"

"Nope," he said, because it was true.

Socializing was fine—normal even. But if drinks and nachos led to sex…well, he definitely had a problem with that.

Some of what he was thinking must have shown on his face, because Garrett took pity on him. "She's not sleeping with Roger or Marty."

"How do you know?"

"Because Roger is over there—" he nodded toward a table on the other side of the room "—with Liz, and Marty is married. And gay."

It was the latter revelation that drew his attention back to his brother. "Where did you get this information?"

"From Roger via Crosby."

"When?"

"I don't remember exactly," Garrett hedged, which was a pretty clear indication to Dean that his brothers had been sitting on the information for a while.

"Were you ever going to tell me?"

"Of course we were, but—"

"But you decided to keep me in the dark for your own amusement?" Dean asked, rightfully annoyed with all his siblings.

"Not for our amusement," Garrett denied. "To get you to finally acknowledge your feelings for Susanna."

Who'd also withheld some pertinent information, Dean realized with irritation.

Yes, she'd told him that her costar was in a relationship, but she hadn't said that he was married. And she certainly hadn't mentioned that he had a husband.

"Why didn't she tell me?"

He didn't realize he'd asked the question out loud until he saw his brother shrug.

"You're missing the point," Garrett said. "And it's not about Marty or Roger or any other guy—it's that you don't want Susanna to be with anyone else because you're in love with her."

Tyler had said the same thing, and Dean had wanted to deny it. Because getting naked with Susanna was one thing—and a very enjoyable one, at that—but falling in love was something else entirely.

"Did you see a ghost on the haunted bar stool?" Garrett asked, turning to look at the empty seat. "Your face seemed to go white all of a sudden."

"I'm fine," Dean said.

Fine and definitely *not* in love.

Because there was no going back after falling in love, and Dean wasn't willing to risk his friendship with Susanna—or her relationship with his parents and siblings—for the unlikely and elusive possibility of something more.

"Why don't you have another beer?" Garrett suggested. "I'll drive back to the ranch."

Dean decided that was the most sensible thing his brother had said all night.

When Crosby walked into his office Monday morning, Dean decided it was as good a time as any to confront his brother about the secrets he'd kept. But Crosby launched an offensive first, demanding to know, "What the hell did you do?"

Dean was taken aback by his brother's tone, but he leaned back in his chair and steepled his fingers to portray casual interest rather than concern. "I'm going to need more information than that if you expect me to answer your question."

"Susanna gave her notice."

"Wait—what?" Dean was no longer feigning ignorance. "Notice about what?"

Crosby shook his head. "She's quitting her job."

"No way," he said, not just stunned but shaken right down to his boots. "I don't believe it."

He didn't want to believe it.

"You think I'd make something like this up?" his brother challenged.

Of course he wouldn't. And yet—

"Susanna loves her job here," he pointed out, confident that it was true.

"That's what we all thought," Crosby agreed. "But apparently she's decided that it's time to try something new."

He swallowed. "Did she say what that something new was?"

Was she planning to go to California? Or New York?

The possibility made him feel ill.

"She didn't *say* anything," Crosby admitted. "I found a copy of her resignation letter in the printer." He held up a sheet of paper.

If she'd actually written a letter, this wasn't his brother overreacting or misunderstanding. It was really real.

Dean swallowed. "Can I see it?"

Crosby dropped the single page on his desk.

Dean quickly scanned the contents.

"I don't get it," Crosby said. "Susanna's always struck me as a practical woman—not someone who would quit one job before she had another one lined up."

But according to the contents of the letter, that's exactly what she was doing—moving away from Bronco "to explore other options."

His brother was right, Dean acknowledged. Susanna was practical. And hardworking and smart. She was also beautiful and sexy and fun, sweet and caring and compassionate. And those were only a few of the many reasons that he loved her.

He gripped the edge of the desk as the truth hit him like a sucker punch.

He loved her!

It was no longer just a niggling possibility but an undeniable fact.

When he'd been with Whitney, when she'd been making plans for their life together, he couldn't imagine a future for them together. But now, thinking about the years ahead, it was Susanna he pictured beside him. And he didn't want to imagine a future without her in it.

Garrett had warned Dean that there would be a hole in his life if he let Susanna go, and he knew just where it would be—in the middle of his chest, where his heart was beating a little too fast right now.

"Why would she do this?" Crosby asked.

Because I told her to.

But no way in hell was Dean going to confess *that* to his brother.

Instead he shook his head, as if he didn't know.

As if he hadn't quite possibly made the biggest mistake of his life.

But what if leaving Bronco was the best option for Susanna? Didn't he want her to be happy?

Of course he did.

But he wanted her to be happy in Bronco.

With him.

"Dean?"

He yanked his attention back to his brother.

"Are you okay?" Crosby asked.

"Yeah. I'm fine."

But it was a lie. He wasn't fine. He was freaking out at the thought that he might lose Susanna forever.

Then their father walked into the office.

"What the hell is going on with our Susanna?" Hutch demanded.

Our Susanna.

Dean wasn't surprised by his father's word choice. From the first day that Susanna started work at Abernathy Meats, she'd fit right in, almost as if she was part of the family.

Because his mom and dad and all his brothers loved her.

And he loved her, too.

His Susanna.

"Crosby told you about her resignation letter?" he guessed.

"I don't know what she's thinking," Hutch grumbled. "But she can't leave."

Tell her that, Dean wanted to say. *Appeal to her sense of loyalty and her affection for the family. Make her stay.*

Because he wanted his dad to beg so that he wouldn't have to.

"Did she say anything to you about this?" Hutch demanded.

Dean shook his head.

"Well, you need to talk to her."

"Why me?"

"Because she'll listen to you."

"I don't know that that's true," Dean hedged, though he was very much afraid it was—and that the resignation letter in his hand was proof that she already had.

Chapter Sixteen

Susanna had been tempted to take the two weeks before Christmas off so that she could focus exclusively on the play, but she knew that if she did so, the work would only pile up in her absence and she'd have that much more to do when she went back after Christmas. And now that she'd made the decision to give her notice, she was glad she was in the office, so that she could talk to Hutch about her decision.

She'd drafted a resignation letter, to make it official, but she intended to hand-deliver it to the boss who had been so great to her for the past eight years. Except that when she went to the printer to retrieve the letter, it was gone.

"I heard you gave your notice."

She turned to face Dean, panic swelling inside her. "What? No, I didn't."

"You wrote a resignation letter."

Ohmygod. "*You* took my letter?"

"Actually, Crosby found it."

"I didn't mean for anyone to *find* it," she said, snatching the page from his hand. "I wanted to take it to your dad myself."

"But…why?"

"Why?" she echoed. "Because I owe him that much."

"I meant, why did you write the letter?"

"Should we start with the fact that you told me to go?" she suggested.

He winced. "I never told you to quit your job."

"So you expected that I'd somehow manage to continue working for Abernathy Meats from California or New York?" she challenged.

"So you *are* leaving."

She sighed. "No. I mean, of course I'm leaving— that's why I wrote the letter. But I'm only going to Bozeman."

"Is there a theater community in Bozeman that I don't know about?"

"I certainly hope so. But I want to do more than just perform onstage," she told him.

"Tell me what you want, Susanna. Maybe I can help make your dreams come true."

She shook her head, her heart breaking. If only he knew that he was the only one who could. But she'd made up her mind to move away, to move on. To get over her crush on Dean once and for all and perhaps, someday, fall in love with someone else. Someone who would want to be with her as much as she wanted to be with him. "I don't think you can."

"What if…what if I asked you not to go?"

Her foolish and hopeful heart swelled inside her chest, imagining that he wanted her to stay because he wanted to be with her, then deflated again when she remembered that he'd told her to go. *To show the world what you're capable of.*

"Your parents must really want me to stay if you're here to change my mind."

"Of course they want you to stay. We all want you to stay. But that isn't what this is about."

"Isn't it?"

"I'm trying to tell you how I feel," he said, sounding frustrated.

"How do you feel?" she challenged.

He swallowed. "I… I care about you, Susanna."

"I know you do." She also knew that he'd meant the words to be reassuring, but instead, she couldn't help feeling disappointed. Because she knew that Hutch and Hannah and Garrett, Weston, Crosby and Tyler all cared about her, too—and she cared about them.

But she loved Dean, and she wanted him to love her back.

"And you don't need to feel responsible or guilty because I've decided to leave town," she told him now. "I'm not running away because you broke my heart. I'm just moving on."

"Are you saying that you don't have feelings for me?" he challenged.

If she was really brave, she'd tell the man she loves the truth about her feelings.

With Callie's words echoing in the back of her mind, Susanna drew in a deep breath, met his gaze evenly and said, "I love you, Dean. I've loved you for eight years, but I've finally realized that I deserve to be with someone who can love me back."

"Susanna—"

She held up a hand. "Please, don't say anything else."

"But—"

"No." She shook her head for added emphasis as she valiantly fought against the tears that threatened. "Just go."

Susanna was proud of herself—for finally telling Dean the truth about her feelings and for managing to hold back the tears until she got home. But Joyce took one look at her daughter and opened her arms, and enfolded in the familiar comfort of her warm embrace, Susanna completely fell apart.

Her mom steered her into the living room and onto the sofa, somehow without loosening her hold. And she let Susanna cry it out, without asking any questions or offering any useless platitudes.

"I gave notice at my job today," she confided when she'd pulled herself together enough to be able to speak.

"Well, good," Joyce said.

Susanna's surprise must have shown on her face, because her mom continued, "It was a good job and the Abernathys treated you well, but it couldn't have been easy, seeing Dean at work every day."

"You know...how I feel about Dean?"

"I know." Joyce tucked a stray hair behind Susanna's ear. "But does he?"

She nodded. "I finally told him."

"And these tears are because he doesn't feel the same way?" her mom guessed.

She nodded again.

"Well, I have some news that might be a silver lining," Joyce said. "Mabel Keller came into the store today and told me that she's thinking of moving to Texas, to be closer to her grandkids, and she wondered if you might be interested in managing the theater."

The possibility was almost tempting enough to make Susanna consider staying in Bronco. But she'd already come to the same realization as her mom, that she was never going to get over Dean if she saw him every day—or if there was even the possibility that she might see him on any given day. And while managing the old theater was, in many ways, her dream job, she couldn't do it.

"Actually, I've been looking at job postings in Bozeman."

"Oh."

"I just feel like I need a completely fresh start," Susanna said, pleading for her mom to understand.

Joyce nodded, though her eyes had gone misty now. "You need to do what's best for you."

"Bozeman's really not that far."

"Not too far," her mom agreed, trying to sound upbeat.

"And maybe, now that I'm finally moving out, you'll move on with your life, too—with Ted."

"I'm quite happy with my life the way it is."

"But you're happier with Ted," Susanna said. "I know, because I've seen the two of you together."

"He's a good man," Joyce agreed. "And while I would never say that a woman needs a romantic partner, loving—and being loved—makes life complete, and that's what I want for you.

"And I'm sorry," her mom continued, "because I know I encouraged your affections for Dean, because I honestly believed that he was a man who could love you the way you deserve to be loved."

"I guess we were both wrong there," Susanna said, attempting to smile even as tears filled her eyes again.

Joyce hugged her tight. "I still think you should talk to Mabel before you start applying for jobs in Bozeman, but I'll support you, whatever you decide to do."

Dean had left Susanna's office, because it was what she'd asked him to do. And because he needed time to regroup and figure out a plan—fast—to change her mind about leaving Bronco.

And while she was still at the office, he headed over to the high school.

It wasn't until he got there and saw the empty parking lot that he remembered it was only five days before Christmas and the students—and teachers—

were off for their winter break. Which meant that he was going to have to track Marty Trujillo down at home.

"You're not Marty," he said, when the door was opened by someone else.

"I'm Marty's husband, Brian," the other man told him.

"I'm sorry to intrude," Dean told him. "But I really need to talk to Marty. Is he here?"

Brian pulled the door wider to allow Dean to see down the hall and into the kitchen, where Marty was sitting at the table eating something out of a bowl.

"I'm interrupting your meal," he realized.

"We eat a bigger lunch on performance days, so that Marty doesn't go onstage with a full stomach."

"Don't be sharing trade secrets with strangers," Marty admonished his husband.

"I assumed he was a friend of yours."

"We've never actually been introduced," Dean admitted.

Brian raised his brows at that.

"I'm Dean Abernathy."

"He's a friend of Susanna's," Marty explained.

"I see." Brian narrowed his gaze on the visitor before turning his head to glance at his husband again. "Is he allowed to come in?"

"I am curious to know what compelled him to track me down at home," Marty said.

"That's a yes," Brian interpreted for Dean, moving away from the door to allow him entry.

He stepped inside and wiped his boots on the mat.

Marty pushed away from the table and met him in the foyer.

"I screwed up," Dean said, without preamble. "As I'm sure Susanna told you at Doug's the other night."

"Your name might have come up in conversation," the other man acknowledged, clearly not willing to break Susanna's confidence to give away anything more than that.

"But I have a plan to fix things," he continued.

"That plan better include the grandest of grand gestures," Marty told him.

"Actually, I was thinking of something a little bit smaller," Dean admitted. "But I'm going to need your help."

Marty looked at his partner.

"We've always been suckers for a happy ending," Brian admitted to Dean. "So tell us what we can do to help make this one happen."

Dean didn't want to wait until the evening performance was over to see Susanna again, so after he finished his consultation—and shopping excursion—with Marty and Brian, he headed over to her mom's house. He'd hoped to avoid crossing paths with Joyce, but luck was not on his side.

And unlike the last time he stopped by, she didn't seem the least bit happy to see him.

"I don't know why you're here," she said. "But I think you've done enough damage."

"What did I do?" he asked cautiously.

She sniffed. "My daughter's suddenly got it in her head that she needs to move to Bozeman, and you don't even realize that you're the reason she's leaving."

"I hope that's not true," Dean said. "And I hope I can give her a reason to stay."

"I hope so, too," Joyce said. "She's upstairs. Packing."

Packing?

Dean felt his heart splat at his feet, but he paused to take his boots off before taking the stairs two at a time.

Susanna was standing at a writing desk by the window, wrapping presents, and he exhaled a grateful sigh.

"Your mom said you were packing."

She glanced up, her expression a combination of surprise and dismay. "Dean. What are you doing here?"

"Your mom said you were packing," he said again.

"Are you sure she didn't say *wrapping*?"

"I'm sure," he said, because if she'd said wrapping, he wouldn't have panicked at the thought that Susanna's departure was somehow imminent.

"In any event, your timing is good," she said. "I finished your presents when I got home from work. They're in the dining room, with sticky notes on each one so that you can fill out the tags."

"I didn't come for the presents," he told her.

Truthfully, he'd completely forgotten about them. He'd forgotten everything else in his urgency to fix his relationship with Susanna. But the fact that she hadn't forgotten, that she'd still help him out after everything he'd said and done—or *not* said and *not* done—proved once again that she was an amazing woman. Certainly a much better woman than he deserved, though he was going to do his darnedest to change that.

"So why are you here?"

"To ask you to stay."

She affixed a bow to the top of a box. "Haven't we done this dance already?"

"Actually, that's one thing we haven't done," he noted. "Danced. Or gone on a real date."

"I appreciate the effort," she said. "But I've got things to finish before I head over to the theater."

"First, can I give you this?" He thrust a brightly wrapped box topped with a fat green bow at her.

"Thank you." She managed a smile. "I'll put it under the tree and—"

"No," he interrupted. "You have to open it now."

"My mom has a pretty strict rule about waiting until Christmas to open presents," she reminded him.

"It's not really a Christmas present," he said. "It's more of a…forever present."

What did that mean? Susanna wondered.

Was the gift something to take with her—to help her remember him when she was living in Bozeman? She appreciated the gesture, but she didn't need a token or memento to remember him. No matter where she went, she would always carry him in her heart.

But since it seemed to mean a lot to him, she finally nodded. "Okay, I'll open it now."

She carefully pried the bow from the top and set it aside, then turned the box over, looking for a seam in the paper. "You did a great job with the wrapping."

"Actually, I had it wrapped in the store," he confessed sheepishly.

She slid the box out of the paper and lifted the lid. "Oh."

She recognized it immediately, of course, because it was a duplicate of the heart-shaped ornament that Noel gave to Holly in the final scene of *A Christmas Wish*.

"Where did you get this?" she asked, since that seemed like a safer question than the one she really wanted to ask.

"At Granny's Attic," he said, naming a local shop that specialized in seasonal and gift items. "Marty told me that's where the prop guy picked up the ornament that Noel gives to Holly at the end of the play, to symbolize that he's offering her his heart."

Which she knew, of course, because she not only played the role of Holly, she'd written the script.

"So why are you giving it to me?" she finally asked.

"I hoped it would be obvious," he said.

"I think I'm going to need you to spell it out."

"It's a symbol of my heart," he said.

"That you're giving to me to take to Bozeman?"

"God, I hope not." He scrubbed his hands over his face. "I'm not doing a very good job of this, am I?"

"I guess it depends on what you're trying to do," she said.

"I'm trying to tell you that I don't want you to go to Bozeman. Or California or New York. I want you to stay here in Bronco. With me. Because if you leave, you'll be taking my heart with you—and not just the one that you're holding in your hand."

And her own began to fill with hope again.

"I think I'm starting to get the picture," she said.

"Is it a picture of you and me?" he asked. "Because that's what I want—for us to be together. Because I love you."

And with those last three words—the three words she'd never expected to hear him say—Susanna completely melted.

"It's what I want, too," she said, her heart overflowing now. "But…after the night we spent together at the theater, you seemed eager to put me back in the friend zone."

"Because I didn't know what I wanted," he confided, drawing her into his arms. "Because I was an idiot."

"Yes, you were," she agreed, with a smile that assured him he was already forgiven.

"I didn't realize how much you meant to me until I was faced with the possibility of losing you forever," he continued. "You aren't just the center of my world, Susanna, you are my world. You're everything to me."

Her eyes filled.

"Damn," she said, brushing impatiently at the tears that spilled onto her cheeks. "I promised myself that I was done crying for today."

"I made you cry," he realized. "Susanna, I'm so sorry."

"Don't tell me you're sorry," she said. "Tell me again that you love me."

"I love you. For now and forever."

"That's good to know," she said, drawing his mouth down to hers. "Because I love you, too."

On Christmas Eve, Susanna went with Dean to the Flying A for the legendary dessert party. It was, as she'd remarked to Hannah a few weeks earlier, a family event, and though Susanna had known all of Dean's family for as long as she'd known him, this was the first time she would be at an event *with* Dean, and she wasn't entirely sure how that would change the dynamic.

She needn't have worried. His parents and brothers all greeted her warmly, sincerely happy to see her—and glad to learn that she was staying in Bronco, even if she was planning to apply for Mabel Keller's job managing the theater—and not the least bit surprised to learn that she and Dean were finally together.

"We've been placing bets on how long it would take our clueless brother to figure out that you were the right woman for him," Tyler confessed to a stunned Susanna.

"I put my money on a New Year's Eve epiphany," Garrett admitted.

"I had New Year's Day," Weston chimed in.

"I didn't figure he'd come around before Valentine's Day," Crosby said.

"No one told me about the pool," Hutch grumbled. "Though I probably would have put my money on the Fourth of July, only because he has trouble figuring out what he wants sometimes."

"I picked Christmas," Tyler said smugly. "Which isn't going to make me rich, but I'm happy to claim the bragging rights that go with winning."

"You might have won the bet," Dean said, sliding an arm across Susanna's shoulders. "But I won the girl."

"That's okay," Tyler said, drawing Callie close. "I've got one of my own."

"And I'm perfectly happy flying solo," Weston said.

"Which likely means that by next Christmas, we'll be placing bets on you," Garrett suggested.

"I don't want to hear any more talk about gambling," Hannah admonished her sons. "Especially when the stakes are so high."

Crosby rolled his eyes. "It was five bucks, Mom."

"I wasn't referring to your money but your hearts,"

she told him, before disappearing into the kitchen to cut more cranberry bars.

Dean was reluctant to leave Susanna's side for a moment—who knew what stories his brothers would tell her in his absence?—but he whispered, "Be right back," in her ear and followed his mom for a private word.

"Do you need a hand?" he asked.

"Thanks, but no," she told him, arranging the squares on a glossy plate decorated with holly leaves and berries around the rim. "This is hardly a two-person job. Go, be with Susanna."

"I will," he said. "But first, I wanted to be sure that you're okay with me and Susanna."

"Are you kidding?" She wiped her fingers on a towel and turned to face him. "You know that I love Susanna, and I'm *thrilled* to see the two of you together."

"What about your plans to nudge Crosby in her direction?"

"Oh, Dean." She gave him an indulgent smile. "You've always been so predictable."

"I'm not following."

"I never really thought that Susanna and Crosby would be a good match, but I hoped that if you thought I was trying to play matchmaker for Susanna, you'd finally see that *you* were her perfect match."

"You're as sneaky as my brothers," he said, and told her about the information they'd withheld from him.

"Don't be mad," she urged.

He snagged a square. "How can I be mad when your collective machinations helped me see what I couldn't—that Susanna is the perfect woman for me?"

Hannah only smiled as she added another square to the plate to replace the one that was now in his mouth.

They didn't stay late at the dessert party. Just long enough for Dean to ensure that Susanna experienced the unprecedented sugar high that he'd promised her—had it really only been two weeks earlier?

Of course, he used her busy schedule over the past few weeks as an excuse to cut out early, which didn't fool anyone. Because instead of taking Susanna home, he took her to his cabin, so that they could steal a few hours alone.

"You have a Christmas tree," she noted with surprise, when she saw the silhouette illuminated by colorful lights through his front window. "I assumed, since you spend most of the holidays at the main house, you wouldn't worry about decorating your own place."

"And you'd be right," he told her. "But I know how much you love Christmas, and I knew that I wanted to bring you here tonight, so I decided to add a few festive touches."

"Well, the tree looks wonderful," she told him.

"Wait until you see what I've done in the bedroom," he said, with a wink.

She laughed softly. "Is that the cowboy version of 'Do you want to come up to my loft and see my sketches'?"

He shrugged. "Well, I don't have a loft and I don't sketch."

"So show me your bedroom."

"I was going to at least offer you a drink first," he said.

"I had more than enough to drink—and eat—at your mom and dad's house," she assured him. "What I want right now is you."

And there was no way Dean was going to argue with *that*, so he took her hand and led her down the hall to his bedroom.

"I've dreamed of you here," he said, pausing just inside the doorway. "Every night since the night in the theater."

"You have?"

He nodded. "Incredibly vivid dreams of all the things I wanted to do with you."

"I've dreamed of you, too," she admitted. "Even before that night."

"I wanted you before then," he confided now. "Even when I told myself I shouldn't."

"Why did you think you shouldn't want me?"

"Because you're nine years younger than me. Because we're friends."

"I'll always be nine years younger than you," she

acknowledged. "But there's no reason we can't be friends *and* lovers."

Dean pulled her close. "I do love you, Susanna."

She lifted her arms to link her hands behind his head and brought his mouth down to hers, whispering against his lips, "Show me."

Chapter Seventeen

Dean kissed her then, in his patient and thorough way, until all the bones in her body felt as if they would melt away and leave her in a puddle on his rustic hardwood floor.

"I forgot something," he said, and stepped away from her briefly to light the trio of pillar candles on the table beside the bed.

The candles were deep red in color, their bases wrapped in festive ribbon decorated with miniature pine cone accents.

"Were you referring to the candles when you implied that you'd decorated your bedroom?" she asked, seeing no other obvious signs of the holiday season around the room.

"No, I was referring to the mistletoe," he said, and pointed to the ceiling.

Susanna looked up to discover no less than a dozen sprigs of the green plant tacked up around the room.

She laughed softly. "You weren't taking any chances, were you?"

"I just didn't want to waste any time maneuvering you to exactly the right spot so that I could kiss you," he said.

"And look at that," she mused. "We're under the mistletoe."

"So we are," he agreed, and kissed her again.

As his lips moved over hers, his hands skimmed up her back, tracing the line of her spine, making her shiver. He found the zipper at the back of her neck and slowly inched it downward. When it was completely unzipped, he eased the garment over her shoulders and tugged the sleeves down her arms, then pushed the fabric over her hips so that it pooled at her feet.

"Merry Christmas to me," he said, as his gaze skimmed over her, clad now in only a red satin bra with lace trim and matching hip hugger panties.

"I was in a festive mood, too," she said.

"I thought you looked spectacular in that dress," he said now. "But you look even better out of it."

It wasn't just the sincerity in his tone but the heat in his eyes as they moved over her body that convinced Susanna he meant the words. That when he looked at her, he didn't see hips that were too wide or thighs that didn't gap in the middle. He truly saw—and appreciated—every inch of her curvy body.

"And it's probably a good thing I didn't know what you were wearing beneath it," he continued, "or I might have taken you to my childhood bedroom before we left my mom and dad's house."

"That could have been awkward."

"This is better," he agreed, sliding a finger down a bra strap, from her shoulder to the tiny little bow at the edge of the cup. "I have to say, I really like your lingerie—or at least what I've seen of it so far."

"I like the sensation of silky fabric against my skin," she confided. "But not nearly as much as I like the way it feels when you touch me."

"That's lucky," he said. "Because there's nothing I like as much as touching you."

To prove it, he traced the edge of her bra, his fingertip lightly skimming the swell of one breast, dipping into the hollow, then up again and over the other.

"Your skin is so soft," he murmured. "So perfect."

He found the clasp at her back and unhooked it, then drew the straps down her arms and tossed the garment aside. Then he tugged her panties over her hips and down her legs.

She'd barely registered the fact that he'd dropped to his knees in front of her before his hands were sliding up the backs of her legs, holding her steady as his mouth found her center.

She gasped with shock as his tongue stroked the ultrasensitive nub, making her breath catch and her muscles tremble. He nibbled and licked and sucked, and the myriad of sensations that assailed her was almost too much.

She'd had other lovers, but never had she been with a man so focused on her pleasure. And while she'd always enjoyed sex, never had she experienced as much pleasure as she'd felt with this man.

And just when she thought there couldn't possibly be any more, Dean proved otherwise.

Again and again.

"Dean…please…"

He stopped what he was doing only long enough to nudge her closer to the bed, allowing her to perch on the edge of the mattress, while he continued his ministrations. His hands were firm on her hips, holding her still while he did wonderfully wicked things with his mouth, every flick of his tongue driving her closer to the edge of oblivion. Her fingers fisted in the quilted cover, desperate for something to hold on to as her mind spun and her body flew.

When she was shuddering with the aftereffects of her climax, he eased away from her long enough to strip away his own clothes. Then he drew her farther up onto the mattress, quickly sheathed himself with a condom and lowered himself over her. Bracing his weight on his forearms, he nudged her legs apart and brushed his lips over hers.

"Now," she said. "Please."

He didn't make her wait any longer. In one deep stroke, he buried himself inside her, filling and fulfilling her. And it was almost like the morning at the theater, only so much better.

Because this time, she knew it was more than a stolen moment.

This time, she was making love with the man she loved—a man who loved her, too.

She hadn't intended to fall asleep, and didn't realize that she'd done so until she was awakened by Dean's kiss.

"Merry Christmas, sweetheart," he said, when her eyes flickered open.

She smiled as she snuggled closer to his warmth. "I must have been a very good girl this year, because you are the best present ever."

He chuckled softly. "You were very, very good. And, at the same time, very, very naughty."

She felt heat rush to her cheeks, because apparently she had no inhibitions about doing all kinds of things with him in the dark, but she couldn't talk about them without blushing like a virgin.

"What time is it?"

He glanced over her shoulder to the glowing numbers of the clock on his bedside table. "Three eighteen."

She sighed regretfully. "I have to go. I promised my mom that I'd be there on Christmas morning."

"I know. And since it's technically Christmas and morning, we need to get dressed so that I can take my princess home before she turns into a pumpkin."

"It was actually the coach that turned back into the pumpkin," Susanna told him.

"What?"

She shook her head, smiling. "Never mind."

Because the details didn't really matter.

What mattered was that she was finally getting her own happy ending.

Susanna stared at the long line of vehicles parked end to end in the driveway of the Ambling A, the ranch owned by Hutch Abernathy's brother, George, and George's wife, Angela. And she decided it was a good thing that she was accustomed to the spotlight, because she suspected that it was going to be focused on her as soon as they walked through the door.

"I feel as if I should apologize in advance," Dean said, speaking to both Susanna and Joyce, who was sitting in the back seat with an enormous poinsettia on her lap—a gift for the holiday hosts.

Though Susanna had offered to drive herself and her mom, Dean had insisted on trekking into town again—after making the round trip only a few hours earlier to return Susanna home so that she could spend Christmas morning with Joyce. She wondered now if his insistence had been less about chivalry and more about making sure she didn't change her mind when she saw how many people were there.

"My family can be a lot to take sometimes," Dean continued. "And it looks like the whole family is here."

"Well, of course," Joyce said. "Because it's Christmas, and Christmas is a celebration of faith and family."

Susanna was grateful that he'd included her mom

in his invitation, so that Joyce wouldn't be alone. Next year, she suspected that her mom would be spending at least part of the time with Ted's family, who had welcomed her with open arms, but this year they were celebrating together, as they'd done for as long as Susanna could remember.

Dean gave her hand a gentle squeeze as they stepped into the house. "Don't say I didn't warn you."

The whole family was a lot of people, Susanna realized.

"A packed house," she murmured, as Dean helped her out of her coat.

She was acquainted with several of his cousins already and introduced now to several more. In addition to the usual cast of Abernathys, there were representatives from the most recently discovered branch of the family, which included Winona Cobbs, who'd been in a relationship with Dean's great-grandfather a long, long time ago. Winona was with her daughter, Daisy/Dorothea, granddaughter, Wanda, and great-grandchildren Vanessa—with her fiancé, Jameson John, and Evan—with his wife, Daphne.

Eventually Susanna made her way through the whole group, exchanging pleasantries and holiday greetings with all of Dean's relatives.

"Your play was every bit as wonderful as I knew it would be," Winona said, when Susanna reached her side.

"And you were right, too, that life sometimes imitates art," she acknowledged.

The old woman sent her a conspiratorial wink. "But even better than a happy ending is a happy beginning, and I can tell that you and Josiah's great-grandson are finally beginning yours."

"Thank you," Susanna said, as she lowered herself onto the floor near the Christmas tree, beside Dean and next to Tyler's fiancée.

"How are Maggie's puppies doing?" Callie, playing pat-a-cake with thirteen-month-old Maeve, who was sitting on her lap, asked Daphne, seated across from them.

"They're growing fast and will be ready to go to their new families by Valentine's Day," the owner of Happy Hearts said.

"Have you chosen adoptive homes for all of them then?" Susanna asked her.

Daphne nodded. "And it wasn't easy, because we had a lot of applications."

Dean, who'd been watching her closely, obviously read the disappointment on Susanna's face.

"You wanted one," he realized.

"Yes," she admitted. "And no."

He lifted a brow.

"At first I did, because I totally fell in love with them when they were born and I had every intention of going to Happy Hearts and filling out an application," she explained. "But then, when I was planning to move to Bozeman, it didn't seem to make a lot of sense to adopt a puppy that might be traumatized by a big move, especially not knowing what my living arrangements or work schedule would be."

"Let's not talk about your plan to move to Bozeman," Hutch suggested.

"Thankfully it was a short-lived plan," Hannah said, patting her husband's arm reassuringly.

"And Susanna is staying right here," Joyce added.

"Getting back to the subject of puppies for a moment," Dean said, reaching to retrieve a gift bag from under the tree. "I have a little something for Susanna."

Since it was Christmas, she had no compunction about opening this gift, and quickly dispensed with the decorative tissue to see what was inside.

It was…a plush toy?

She pulled it out of the bag and laughed softly. "Ohmygoodness," she said. "It looks just like Maggie's puppies."

"You have no idea how hard it was to find an Australian shepherd plush toy," he told her. "If you want a golden Lab or beagle or Chihuahua—no problem. They're everywhere. But an Australian shepherd? Not so much."

"Well, I appreciate the effort," she said, hugging the toy close to her chest. "And the gift." She leaned over to touch her lips to his cheek. "Thank you."

"And in February, I'm going to take you to Happy Hearts to pick up Maggie Junior or Holly or whatever you decide to name your real puppy."

Susanna's eyes grew wide. "Really?" She shifted

her attention momentarily to Daphne. "We're getting one of the puppies?"

The other woman nodded, smiling. "I was so grateful to learn that you sheltered Maggie from the storm that night, I impulsively promised the pick of the litter to Dean when he called to tell me that the puppies had been born."

"Apparently having forgotten that she'd already promised the pick of the litter to Boone Dalton at the tree lighting," her husband, Evan, noted.

Daphne gave a sheepish shrug.

"It's probably a good thing there are eight puppies," Dean's cousin Gabe remarked. "Since it seems that you promised one to everyone who helped Maggie find her way home after one of her great escapes."

Everyone chuckled at that, then Susanna's expression grew serious. "I guess, in some ways, it was lucky my car broke down so that I ended up back at the theater that night. Otherwise no one would have been there to offer Maggie shelter from the storm."

Dean linked their hands together. "Lucky for Maggie," he agreed. "And even luckier for me, because that's the night I realized the truth of my feelings for you."

"Oh," Hannah sighed. "That's so romantic."

"It's also revisionist history," Susanna said.

"I didn't say I embraced my feelings that night," Dean acknowledged, with a playful wink.

"Because he wouldn't be a man if he didn't desperately try to regain his balance when he realized he was falling in love," Hutch said, in his son's defense.

When various family members finally stopped chuckling, Dean shook his head. "I obviously didn't think this through…"

"Because falling in love messes with your brain," Weston said.

"What do you know about falling in love?" his mom chided.

"Just enough to know to avoid it," he assured her.

"I certainly didn't consider that there would be a running commentary from the peanut gallery," Dean said.

"Hey!" his brother—and several others—protested.

"Didn't think what through?" Susanna asked Dean, ignoring the peanut gallery.

He tapped the fabric collar around the plush dog's throat, drawing her attention to the shiny metal tag— and the even shinier diamond ring hanging beside it.

She sucked in a breath, her gaze lifting to his.

"Are you…" The rest of the words stuck in her throat when she noticed he was now on one knee.

"I'm asking you to marry me, Susanna."

Her eyes filled with happy tears, and though she wanted to respond with a resounding yes, she felt compelled to say, "This is happening kind of fast, don't you think?"

"Only if eight years is fast," he said dryly.

She laughed softly, but still, she hesitated. "Are you sure?"

"I wouldn't be asking if I wasn't sure," he told her.

The sincerity in his tone echoed the emotion in his eyes, but she couldn't forget that he'd been engaged before. And while her heart was doing a happy dance inside her chest, there was a tiny part of her that worried that if she said yes, this engagement might end the same way.

"I never asked Whitney to marry me," he said quietly, as if privy to her innermost thoughts. "We got engaged because it was what she wanted and because I didn't see any reason not to go along with her plans."

He took her hands in his. "I'm asking you to marry me because I love you with my whole heart, because I want to make plans with you, and because I want to spend every day of the rest of our lives together."

"In that case, I'm saying yes, because I love you with my whole heart, et cetera."

"Did you really just say *et cetera* in response to my proposal?"

She glanced at the crowd of family around them, every one of them leaning in to better see and hear what was happening. "We've got an audience that wants to see how this story ends. Or at least how it begins," she amended, recalling Winona's words.

So Dean removed the ring from the collar and slid it onto the third finger of Susanna's left hand.

"Oh, Joyce," Hannah said, dabbing at her eyes

with a tissue. "We're going to have so much fun to-gether, planning the wedding."

"You better plan fast," Dean said, speaking to both his mother and future mother-in-law. "Because I don't want a long engagement." Then he turned his attention to his fiancée again. "I want to start our life together as soon as possible."

"That sounds perfect to me," Susanna agreed.

And they sealed their deal with a kiss.

Epilogue

Winona looked on approvingly—and perhaps a little smugly—as Dean and Susanna kissed. Because of course she'd known all along that they were meant to be together. It had just taken them (mostly him!) a while to figure it out. She also knew that they were going to have a long and happy life together.

Unlike Josiah and Winona, whose love—though passionate and real—had been doomed from the start. Her darling Josiah had wanted to pretend otherwise, but Winona had known the truth: that the wealthy Abernathys would never allow their son to marry a nobody from an inconsequential family.

But that knowledge had done nothing to temper her affection. She'd loved Josiah with an intensity that had sustained her through her lifetime. And though she didn't get to see him again until he was near the very end of his life, that visit, after more than seventy-five years apart, had meant the world to her.

Now, nearly a year later, as she looked at the people gathered all around her, her heart was filled with happiness and contentment and love. Along with no small amount of gratitude that Josiah had hidden his diary under the floorboards at the original Ambling A Ranch in Rust Creek Falls, the discovery of which had led to finding their daughter here in Bronco.

Being reunited with her child had given Winona a new lease on life. More, it had given her grandchildren and great-grandchildren. A family, after so many years on her own. A family that continued to expand and grow with every season.

Yes, Winona had much for which to be grateful.

As various conversations swirled around her, she leaned close to whisper to her daughter, "I'm going to get some air."

"Now?" Dorothea asked, sounding surprised.

Or maybe thinking that her ninety-four-year-old mother had lost her marbles.

"I won't be long," she promised.

"Do you want company?"

She shook her head. "No, you stay here with your family."

"They're your family, too," Dorothea reminded her.

Winona smiled. "I know."

And maybe it was foolish to venture out into the cold when her family was all together in the warmth, but she wasn't foolish enough to venture out without being properly attired. It took her a few minutes to bundle up before heading out, because even with a new lease on life, she wasn't as spry or hardy as she used to be. So she took care to ensure her coat was buttoned all the way to the chin, that her hat and gloves were on before she slipped out the back door.

The Ambling A was an impressive piece of property, seeming to spread as far as the eye could see in every direction, and Winona took a moment to get her bearings before she began to walk. The fresh snow looked pretty, but it was arduous to trek through. Of course, the paths to the barns had been cleared, but no one was expected to traipse across the open fields in the middle of winter. But that was the only way to get to the top of hill, which she'd been told had been one of Josiah's favorite spots, and now his final resting place.

When she reached the small, simple headstone, she placed the sprig of holly she carried on top of the snow, beneath his name, and laid her gloved hand on top of the granite. "Merry Christmas, Josiah."

Though she didn't actually expect an answer, she waited a beat, just in case, and tried not to feel too disappointed when the only response was the call of a bird in the distance.

"You lived a good long life," she continued, "and though you've been gone from this world for almost a year now, a part of you lives on through your children and grandchildren and great-grandchildren, and I know you'd be proud of each and every one of them.

"I only recently found my own family, after too many years apart, but I promise you, I'm not going to waste a single minute of the time I have left. And as long as I'm here, I'll look after them all—yours and ours," she promised. "And I hope to be here for a long time yet, because there are a lot of great-grandchildren who might need some help to find their perfect matches, and I've still got a lot of wisdom to share."

As she stepped back, away from the stone, a flash of red color caught her eye.

A cardinal.

It was unlikely that it was the same bird she'd seen outside his window when she'd visited Josiah at Snowy Mountain the previous December. And yet, as she watched the bird fade into the distance, the fleeting image, and the sense of continuity it evoked, filled her with peace.

Smiling, she walked back to the house to rejoin the holiday celebrations.

* * * * *

*Catch up with the rest of the
Montana Mavericks:
The Real Cowboys of Bronco Heights continuity!*

The Rancher's Summer Secret
by New York Times *bestselling author
Christine Rimmer*

For His Daughter's Sake
by USA TODAY *bestselling author
Stella Bagwell*

The Most Eligible Cowboy
by Melissa Senate

Grand-Prize Cowboy
by Heatherly Bell

A Kiss at the Mistletoe Rodeo
by Kathy Douglass

and

Dreaming of a Christmas Cowboy
by Brenda Harlen

*Available now, wherever Harlequin books
and ebooks are sold!*

WE HOPE YOU ENJOYED
THIS BOOK FROM

✦ HARLEQUIN
SPECIAL
EDITION

Believe in love. Overcome obstacles. Find happiness.

Relate to finding comfort and strength in the
support of loved ones and enjoy the journey
no matter what life throws your way.

6 NEW BOOKS AVAILABLE EVERY MONTH!

"I'd like to take you out on a proper date then."

"Okay." Color bloomed in her cheeks. "That would be nice." He leaned in, but she held up a finger. "You should know that since Kirby and the gang outed my pregnancy at the coffee shop, I'm not going to hide it anymore." She pressed a hand to her belly. "I'm wearing a baggy shirt tonight because it seemed easier than fielding questions from the boys, but if we go out, there will be questions. And comments."

"I don't care about what anyone else thinks," he assured her and then kissed her gently. "This is about you and me."

Those must have been the right words, because Emmaline wound her arms around his neck and drew closer. "I'm glad," she said, but before he could kiss her again, she yawned once more.

"I'll walk you to your car."

She mock pouted but didn't argue. "I'm definitely not as fun as I used to be," she told him as he picked up the bags with the leftover supplies to carry for her. "Actually I'm not sure I was ever that fun."

"As far as I'm concerned, you're the best."

After another lingering kiss, Emmaline climbed into her car and drove away. Brian watched her taillights until they disappeared around a bend. The night sky overhead was once again filled with stars, and he breathed in the fresh Texas air. He needed to stay in the moment and remember his reason for being in town and how long he planned to stay. He knew better than to examine the feeling of contentment coursing through him.

One thing he knew for certain was that it couldn't last.

Don't miss
Their New Year's Beginning *by Michelle Major,*
available January 2022 wherever
Harlequin Special Edition books and ebooks are sold.

Harlequin.com